P

Safe Shopping, Safe Cooking, Safe Eating

Dr Richard Lacey was born in London in 1940 and is married with two children. He was educated at Felsted School, Essex, and Jesus College, Cambridge, where he was awarded a BA in 1961 and an MB, B.Chir. in 1964. He received his Ph.D. from the Faculty of Medicine at the University of Bristol. His career began at the London Hospital; while working in the Children's Department there, he gained his Diploma in Child Health. From London he moved to Bristol Royal Infirmary and to the Department of Microbiology at the University of Bristol. In 1974 he left his post as Reader in Clinical Microbiology to go to King's Lynn as Consultant in Infectious Diseases for the East Anglian Regional Health Authority. In 1983 he became Professor of Clinical Microbiology at Leeds University. This post involves responsibility for infection control for the Leeds Western Health Authority. Over the years his published work has appeared in many scientific journals.

He has lectured abroad on many occasions and is Consultant to the World Health Organization for Microbiology. He is a Fellow of the Royal College of Pathologists.

Dr Richard Lacey

Safe Shopping, Safe Cooking, Safe Eating

PENGUIN BOOKS

PENGUIN BOOKS

Published by the Penguin Group
27 Wrights Lane, London W8 5TZ, England
Viking Penguin Inc., 40 West 23rd Street, New York 10010, USA
Penguin Books Australia Ltd, Ringwood, Victoria, Australia
Penguin Books Canada Ltd, 2801 John Street, Markham, Ontario, Canada L3R 1B4
Penguin Books (NZ) Ltd, 182–190 Wairau Road, Auckland 10, New Zealand

Penguin Books Ltd, Registered Offices: Harmondsworth, Middlesex, England

First published 1989
10 9 8 7 6 5 4 3 2 1

Printed and bound in Great Britain by
Richard Clay Ltd, Bungay, Suffolk
Filmset in Monophoto Melior

To Miranda and Gemma

Contents

Acknowledgements

I thank all my colleagues in the Department of Microbiology at the University of Leeds for helpful discussions and my secretary, Hilary Mobbs, for instant typing.

R.L.
April 1989

Introduction

Food poisoning has been on the increase since 1983. Recent publicity over salmonella, listeria and food safety in general shows that the incidence of cases is too high. There is now a real problem; the figures have not generally been exaggerated by the media. Of concern to many people is the fact that over the years in the UK we have managed to control, almost completely, infectious diseases such as the plague, smallpox and diphtheria; even the number of patients infected with tuberculosis is much lower now than it was several years ago. We have both the ability and the resources to control food poisoning, yet we have not shown any real effort to do so.

During 1988 well-known causes of food poisoning such as salmonella reached their highest levels ever recorded. In addition, there appeared a new and potentially very dangerous type of infection from food – listeriosis, an infection linked only recently with an increasing range of foods. One of the effects that the problems with both salmonella and listeria have had is to prompt the Department of Health to issue warnings that vulnerable people should avoid risky foods. There seems little prospect that such advice will be withdrawn soon. The need for this advice is being viewed as an alarming development by many people: certain basic commodities required for living are now safe only for some people. The reason for this predicament is not just that our food is more contaminated than it used to be: our expectation of food availability has changed too. Also listeria has now been found to contaminate foods that had formerly been thought safe.

In the USA the association of listeriosis – the disease caused by the bacterium correctly described as *Listeria monocytogenes* – with food dates back to 1981–3. From that time concern about listeria in food was expressed in some European countries, notably France, Switzerland and West Germany – to be followed, belatedly, by the UK. My group in Leeds has been partly responsible for alerting the public to the danger of listeria (a procedure that has not made us popular with the food industry). Our work started in the spring of 1987. At that time it was becoming evident that there was a policy to privatize catering (or at least to make privatization possible) within the National Health Service, local authority institutions and schools. Because it is impossible to bring in reliably hot food from outside caterers and difficult to make bulk deep-frozen food into meals, as ice crystals cause the ingredients to stick together, the cook–chill method is usually required. Briefly, by this method food is cooked in bulk, chilled and stored at just above freezing point (0–30 °C), transported, assembled into meals, then reheated when required. Any food item is, therefore, heated to moderate temperatures (e.g. 70 °C) before and after several days of cold storage.

By early 1987 American concern about listeriosis was appreciated at scientific conferences but had not appeared in the British scientific journals. We understood at that time that listeria was quite resistant to heating, higher temperatures being needed to kill it than some other food-poisoning bacteria such as salmonella. Furthermore, listeria could flourish in cold conditions, at temperatures as low as 0 °C. It looked as though listeria was perfectly designed to contaminate cook–chill food. From 1987 onwards we also became increasingly aware of the rising incidence of listeriosis that was being attributed to the increasing use of refrigeration in catering.

By now readers will be wondering why, once infection with listeria had been traced to food, no action was taken. One reason for this is that the link between food and illness is often extremely difficult to prove, for two reasons. Unlike salmonella food poisoning, which typically affects simultaneously almost everyone who has eaten contaminated food, listeria affects mainly a few vulnerable people, such as pregnant women. The second difficulty in proving a food source for listeriosis is that the time between eating contaminated food and becoming ill can be anything from five days to six weeks. It is rare for suspect food to be kept for weeks – except, interestingly, in the case of certain cheeses, where the link between listeriosis and the food has been made on several occasions.

We therefore began work on listeria in two main areas. First we studied, in our laboratory, aspects of its growth, survival and recovery after being damaged by heating to various temperatures in different foods. Then we went out to supermarkets to sample food that we suspected might be contaminated with listeria. This work had to be done carefully, as precautions have to be taken against contamination of the food during unwrapping and sampling. Our laboratory in Leeds has long-standing experience in food research, and the work was done mainly by Dr Kevin Kerr and Dr Stephen Dealler, with fatherly advice from Dr Patrick Hayes. Our results showed that about a quarter of cook–chill or 'recipe' meals, many of them poultry-based, were contaminated with listeria.

We published the first findings in the *Lancet* at the end of June 1988. The next event occurred in the middle of August 1988. In addition to teaching and research work, our department is responsible for identifying and preventing infections in patients in Leeds. One of our laboratories has the responsibility of finding the cause of infections in mothers and babies in hospital. On two successive days two pregnant women were admitted to the Clarendon Wing of the General Infirmary in Leeds. They were ill and in the early stages of labour. Unfortunately, both mothers gave birth to babies that did not survive. From both mothers and babies we grew in the laboratory, on the surface of agar gels, a culture of bacterium that produced small, greyish, shiny growths, shown, on further testing, to be *Listeria monocytogenes*. (One of the features of this bacterium is its ability to wriggle almost in somersault fashion; this is known as 'tumbling motility'.) We suspected that the source was food and acted immediately, fearing that the contaminated food might have been thrown away some days before.

The patients were carefully interviewed, one by Dr Kevin Kerr and the other by Dr Stephen Dealler, who asked for precise details of their diet over the previous six weeks. Their homes were then visited and samples taken of all food remains in the refrigerator and waste bin. The patient seen by Dr Stephen Dealler had had a conventional diet during her pregnancy, relying on fresh food and home cooking, supplemented by some canned items. The exception to this was the purchase of a cooked and chilled chicken from a local supermarket five days before admission to hospital. If remains of this chicken could be found, there was a possibility of linking the infection in the patient with the presence of the bacteria in the food. Our luck was in because the chicken carcase was still in its bag in the dustbin, which had missed its regular emptying because of the bank holiday. Dr Stephen Dealler very carefully transferred some meat remains from inside the carcase to fluid for growing bacteria. Subsequently *Listeria monocytogenes* was grown from each of two samples, and the culture appeared to be identical with the bacteria from the patient. Dr Kevin Kerr was successful with the other patient; the listeria was traced to a bottle of refrigerated vegetable rennet used for making junkets.

We realized the potential importance of these findings, since previously the only food items that had been proved to be the source of listeriosis in the UK were cheeses. We then sent all the bacteria to two different laboratories in France, where, by different methods, it was confirmed that the bacteria in the food and the corresponding patients were identical.

These findings were published in the *Lancet* in November 1988, just before the salmonella-in-eggs drama broke. The problems with food were now well and truly launched: salmonella was a household word because of the number of cases, the difficulty of ensuring that the cooking of eggs destroys the bacterium and Mrs Edwina Currie's prominence in the media; listeriosis, a new and nasty disease, threatened to stop cook–chill catering in its tracks. Other worries have also arrived, and many readers are confused and irritated by the contradictory statements of food producers, the government and the Department of Health. In this book I hope to explain the problems, to identify safe eating for everyone, from shop to kitchen to cooker, and also to deal with the increasingly popular and hazardous pursuit of eating out.

PART ONE

FOOD POISONING: THE BACKGROUND

1
How much do you know about food poisoning?

Study the following ten sets of questions. Of five possible answers, one or more may be correct. For answers and comments, see pages 6–8.

QUESTIONS

1 Cooked and raw meat should be stored separately because:

(a) gases given off by the cooked meat might affect the quality of the raw meat.
(b) bacteria can be transferred from the raw meat to the cooked meat.
(c) bacteria can be transferred from the cooked meat to the raw meat.
(d) cooked meat should be stored at a lower temperature than raw meat.
(e) the flavour of cooked meat might be spoilt by blood from the raw meat.

2 An ideal refrigerator temperature is:

(a) between 5 °C and 10 °C.
(b) below 0 °C.
(c) between 3 °C and 8 °C.
(d) between 0 °C and 4 °C.

(e) about 12 °C at the top and 4 °C at the bottom.

3 Which of the following statements concerning salmonella are true?

(a) between 1 and 5 per cent of healthy people carry
the bacterium in their intestines.
(b) it will be destroyed in a boiled egg as long as
the white is firm.
(c) its main natural source is birds.
(d) if the cause of food poisoning, the main effect is
to cause vomiting.
(e) it causes more food poisoning in the summer
than in the winter.

4 Match the corresponding food-poisoning bacteria
(a–e) with their typical food sources (1–5).

(a) *Bacillus cereus*   1 soft cheese
(b) salmonella   2 cream
(c) listeria   3 rice
(d) *Staphylococcus*   4 tinned fish
(e) *Clostridium*   5 turkey
    botulinum

5 What is the recommended temperature of a deep
freeze in the home?

(a) −18 °C to −23 °C.
(b) −15 °C to −20 °C.
(c) +1 °C to −1 °C.
(d) −10 °C to −5 °C.
(e) −40 °C to −30 °C.

6 Which of the general statements about food poisoning are true?

(a) Most of the responsible bacteria are common in the environment.
(b) Reported cases are now about double the numbers of five years ago.
(c) People develop natural immunity to food poisoning as they get older.
(d) Food poisoning produces most distressing symptoms to the very young, the elderly and those ill from other diseases.
(e) Food poisoning should be largely preventable.

7 If, in a warm room, a single bacterium divides into two every twenty minutes, how many will be present after six hours?

(a) 24.
(b) 18.
(c) 420.
(d) About 250,000.
(e) 17,214.

8 Thawing a deep-frozen turkey is done preferably:

(a) outside in warm weather.
(b) in a warm kitchen.
(c) in the top of the refrigerator.
(d) in the bottom of the refrigerator.
(e) on the same day it is to be cooked.

9 Flies, pests and vermin are dangerous in food-preparation areas because:

    (a) they can contaminate food with their own bacteria.

    (b) they can transfer bacteria from raw to cooked food.

    (c) they can transfer bacteria between different items of raw food.

    (d) they can carry salmonella.

    (e) they are difficult to eliminate.

10 Which of the following food products usually contain very few or no bacteria?

    (a) tinned peas.

    (b) frozen peas.

    (c) fresh peas.

    (d) custard powder.

    (e) lemon slice.

ANSWERS

1 (b) is correct. Cooked meat should contain few bacteria immediately after cooking. However, cooked meat readily supports the growth of bacteria if they are transferred to it and the product is kept for some days at temperatures of 10 °C or more (listeria can grow even at 0 °C). The surface of raw meat usually contains moderate numbers of bacteria before cooking.

2 (d) is correct. At temperatures below 0 °C ice crystals can damage the texture of the food, and above 4 °C there is a risk of growth of food-poisoning bacteria. All refrigerators should have built-in thermometers.

6

3 (a), (c) and (e) are true. People tend to be carriers
   possibly for weeks after an illness with salmonella.
   In order to kill salmonella in an egg reliably,
   the yolk must be hard – regrettably! Of our food
   animals and birds, chickens, turkeys and ducks
   may all contain salmonella. The main symptom is
   diarrhoea, not vomiting, because the lower bowel is
   involved rather than the upper. Summer is the
   worst time for salmonella because of kitchen and
   catering errors: food may be left in a warm atmosphere inadvertently.

4 (a) 3; (b) 5; (c) 1; (d) 2; (e) 4. See Chapters 7, 5, 6, 4.

5 (a) is correct. At temperatures above $-18\ ^{\circ}C$ there
   is a greater tendency for enzyme activity to increase with more rapid spoilage of the food. Below
   $-23^{\circ}C$ the cost of maintaining very low temperatures is usually too high for the home.

6 (a), (b), (d) and (e) are all true. Justification for (c)
   has never been made, and it provides a too convenient excuse for poor hygiene.

7 (d) is correct, amazingly! One bacterium becomes
   two bacteria after twenty minutes, four after forty
   minutes and eight after one hour. Thereafter the
   numbers increase eightfold every hour.

8 (d) is correct. Ideally, the turkey should be in a
   container to prevent the dripping of the juices on
   to the fridge floor. If the turkey is in the top of the
   fridge, there is a risk of contamination of food
   items below it. The time needed for thawing may
   be three days. In warm environments thawing will

be quicker, but there is a danger that bacteria will start multiplying between thawing and commencement of cooking, which may not be sufficiently thorough to kill these bacteria or neutralize their toxins (poisons).

9 (a), (b), (c) and (d) are all correct. Their elimination should be possible. No excuse!

10 (a) alone is correct. Frozen peas may contain moderate numbers of harmless bacteria in a state of 'suspension' (deep-freezing rarely destroys bacteria, although it does prevent their growth). Fresh vegetables contain moderate numbers of bacteria, which are killed on cooking. Custard powder and lemon slices can contain moderate numbers of bacteria; hence the need to discard custard after use and to eat lemon slices as soon as possible after purchase.

SCORING

Some of the questions are quite difficult. Score two marks for each correct answer, and subtract one mark for each answer that is wrong. (This is necessary, as otherwise everyone could score full marks by ticking every possible answer.) For example, if for question 1 you stated that (a), (b) and (c) were all correct, you would score nothing for that question because your two marks for the correct answer (b) would be cancelled out by the loss of two marks for the incorrect answers (a) and (c).

The maximum possible score is forty-four, and anything over twenty is pretty good!

2
Bacteria and food poisoning

THE SIZE OF BACTERIA

We are all aware that bacteria are very small – but how small? A typical salmonella bacterium is a rod-shaped structure about 0.4μ (millionths of a metre) wide and 3μ long. Does this enable us to comprehend the size? Perhaps if we identify the minimum number of salmonella in a blob that we can just make out with unaided human vision, we may form an impression of their size. The number is about 10 million, and a pinhead could well carry 100 million salmonella. Since infections from salmonella may be caused by 1 million bacteria or less, and since the bacteria could be dispersed throughout infected food, it follows that we are unable to see the salmonella (or other bacteria that cause food poisoning) in food, although we'll certainly feel their effects! It might be thought that the effects of bacterial growth on contaminated food would be obvious. Unfortunately, this is rarely the case, as it is usually impossible to distinguish the effects of bacterial growth from those of the food's own enzymes, which are capable of causing decomposition from bacterial or fungal action.

So food hygiene depends on arresting the growth of bacteria that cannot be seen. The prevention of food poisoning has to be based on knowledge of bacteria (and other micro-organisms) that can be dangerous and of ways in which the hazards can be lessened. In this chapter we will look at some of the properties of bacteria in general and at the methods of food storage that prevent bacteria from causing poisoning.

First, it has to be accepted as inevitable that all plant and animal life in nature harbours bacteria. For most of the time most of these bacteria are beneficial: two examples illustrate this. One is the presence, on the roots of beans, of bacteria that cause the conversion of nitrogen gas in the air to other nitrogen compounds that are used for growth. The second is the beneficial bacteria in all human intestines without which our normal immunity would not develop. However, if these bacteria escape from the intestine to elsewhere in the body, they can cause infection. It has been estimated that the healthy adult person harbours about 1,000 million million bacteria, that is 10^{15}, and that the total number of bacteria in the world is 10 followed by twenty-five noughts! It follows that almost all the raw food we eat will contain some bacteria, as will some lightly cooked products and processed foods. Indeed, our normal health depends on the eating of certain bacteria to let them take up residence in our intestines and, in so doing, prevent possibly dangerous bacteria from getting a foothold. So our approach to hygiene and safe eating is to ensure that we eat only those bacteria that are beneficial. One of the problems we now have to consider is that to some people some bacteria can be beneficial, or at least neutral in their effect, whereas to other people they may be dangerous. These latter people are the vulnerable members of the community, who must take special care over what they eat.

Before looking in detail at the prevention of the growth of bacteria that cause food poisoning, a myth must be exploded. This is the idea that certain micro-organisms (a general term to include all tiny creatures, including bacteria) deliberately intend to attack and damage us, making us ill. To take an extreme example: if a bacterium were successful in its plan to damage the human host as much as it could, the person would die and so would the bacterium. If we can ascribe any motive to bacteria, it is in their interest to live in unison with us. Sometimes the relationship between the human host and the bacteria is truly symbiotic, in that it benefits both the bacterium and the person. Sometimes the benefit is rather one-sided; the bacterium exploits the available nutrients and space in the human body, but the body derives no obvious benefit. These bacteria are referred to as commensals.

So the few bacteria that poison us do so by chance. Harmful products may be released into food by these bacteria entirely by accident, or they may give the bacteria a means of stopping other bacteria from over-running it. Out of the many thousands of types of bacteria that may harm us, in practice the number of dangerous species (particular types of bacteria) is probably less than twenty. We have sometimes to be rather vague about whether a bacterium is dangerous because it may be safe if eaten in small numbers but dangerous in large numbers. In vulnerable people even small numbers could produce illness. The speed of multiplication of bacteria can therefore be important in deciding whether a contaminated food is dangerous.

THE MULTIPLICATION OF BACTERIA

Bacteria can grow very quickly when warm. Assuming plenty of nourishment is present, let us see, for example, what might happen to one bacterium that has dropped from the air into warm gravy. Let us suppose this gravy is being kept at body temperature, 37 °C, on a warm cooker. For the first hour or so, the single bacterium will adapt itself to enable it to use the gravy as a food. Growth will begin in the second hour; the bacteria will divide as often as every twenty minutes until, after seven hours altogether, there will be 250,000 bacteria. This number of bacteria may well cause food poisoning, and if more than one bacterium contaminated the gravy initially, the dangerous number of bacteria could appear sooner. We can see just how dangerous it is to leave cooked food in a warm atmosphere. Of course, not all bacteria divide every twenty minutes, although one, *Clostridium perfringens*, can divide every eleven minutes under perfect conditions. Bacteria will also not increase as rapidly at lower temperatures. At average room temperatures a dangerous level might be reached in twelve to sixteen hours, and, as temperatures get down to those of refrigeration, there should be no growth of most food-poisoning bacteria (listeria excepted – see Chapter 5).

Readers may be wondering why, if the numbers of bacteria increase so rapidly at ordinary temperatures, we do not live in a dense bacterial fog. The reason is that, sooner or later, nutrients in the food and oxygen in the air run out. Bacteria also die on inanimate surfaces, such as furniture, because they dry out and from exposure to ultra-violet light, which penetrates clouds. (Ultra-violet light, one of the invisible rays of the sun, makes our skin tan and occurs at the 'blue end' of the spectrum.) As a result, the air we breathe usually contains few bacteria. The number of bacteria in food is usually not more than 1,000 million per gram – although if we eat 100 grams of contaminated food, our intake amounts to an extraordinarily high number of bacteria.

HOW FOOD IS PRESERVED

Fresh foods

Since many foods support the growth of bacteria, the techniques of food hygiene aim to stop the growth of those that might be dangerous. Heat is the best-established and probably the most certain way of killing bacteria. It has never been clear whether the prime purpose of cooking food in ancient times was to destroy bacteria, or to alter the flavour, or both. Certainly, the traditional method of cooking fresh food should destroy many food-poisoning bacteria. Vegetables, potatoes, pasta or rice, immersed in boiling water and eaten immediately afterwards, rarely give rise to safety problems. Meat products are not as straightforward. Bacteria are always found on the surface of meat or poultry. With joints of meat, the hanging required for tenderizing lasts several days, during which surface bacteria grow. Cooking an intact joint, steak or other 'natural' piece of meat, or fish and poultry, results in the penetration of heat from the outside, even when we use a microwave oven. Any bacterial contamination of the surface should be readily eliminated. However, salmonella can get 'inside' the meat when, for example, joints are boned and rolled and skewers are pushed into the flesh, taking the bacteria with them. Eviscerating poultry can also result in the spread of salmonella from the gut to contaminate the body cavity of the bird.

When raw meat is processed – through mincing or reassembly into new forms – surface bacteria can become distributed throughout the finished product. In order to destroy these bacteria in the centre of, say, a chicken rissole, a sausage or a burger, considerable heat penetration is needed. A change of colour from a pinkish tinge to a brown colour is a helpful indication of heat penetration but is no guarantee of the destruction of all dangerous bacteria or their toxic products. For this reason careful controls in the manufacture of these processed products is essential.

Canned foods

During canning, foods are cooked at high temperatures (up to 130 °C) and generally for a long time. Canned goods should be safe. They should contain either no bacteria at all or only a few immobilized or dormant spores – these are best viewed as inert forms of bacteria that, though they are capable of growth subsequently, do not themselves cause disease.

There are a few ways in which canning can be dangerous, however. It is possible that contaminating bacteria can get into a can before it is sealed; the seams of the can may split during handling; and rusting, perhaps in a crease on the bottom, may occur, which could permit the entry of bacteria into the can. When buying a can, inspect it carefully for three points: there should be no bad dents; there should be no rust; and neither the top nor the bottom should bulge outwards, which would indicate that gas might be being

14

produced by bacteria multiplying inside. In general the quality control of canning is good, and the risk of food poisoning by canned food is tiny. To the author's knowledge, there has been no such case for ten years in the UK. However, problems did exist in the past, and in a later section the sinister food-poisoning disease botulism will be described.

Perhaps in a different risk category are canned hams – very high temperatures can damage the product. Most canned hams contain nitrite preservatives to aid in the prevention of bacterial growth, and the consumer may consider that he or she would prefer to buy additive-free food, in which case the only answer is to avoid canned ham and some related meats (have a look at the label). It should be pointed out that, over the years, there has been little reason to think that nitrites ingested occasionally constitute a health hazard, although they are certainly not fashionable now!

Sterilized microwave meals

A recent development in convenience foods is packets of prepared ready-to-eat (or 'recipe') meals divided into one or two portions. Unlike most of the usual convenience meals, which are produced by heating to pasteurization temperatures (70 °C) and then kept chilled (0–5 °C – hopefully), these new items, in similar cartons and packaging (labelled 'Long life – no need to refrigerate'), are heat-treated to be sterile, so that they can be stored for up to ten months at ordinary room temperatures. The packets are fairly rigid, so insects and vermin are unlikely to introduce bacteria, but there may be some sort of risk with these foods that is greater than that of canned food. The products, in plastic dishes, are reheated directly and very rapidly in microwaves, whereas the content of a tin has to be spooned into a suitable dish for reheating. Certainly, these new products should have the advantage of little risk of bacterial multiplication during storage and may just set the trend in convenience food. We did confirm that a number of these items were sterile, but we would encourage the manufacturers to look further into the balance of flavour between the principal ingredients and the sauces.

Deep freezing

The purpose of deep freezing is to stop two processes — the growth of micro-organisms and the activity of enzymes in the food itself, which may result in decomposition if storage has to be prolonged. As with canning, deep freezing is a procedure that enables food to be stored for weeks or months, then to be immediately available when required, often on an unpredictable occasion. In the case of listeria the lowest temperature at which a food-poisoning bacterium can grow is 0 °C, but other bacteria can grow at −5 °C and some moulds at −10 °C. The growth of these latter micro-organisms may affect the taste of the food, but it is unlikely to lead to food poisoning. Most deep-freeze temperatures are between −18 °C and −23 °C, which should provide enough margin of safety to ensure that no micro-organisms will grow at all. However, some deep-freeze cabinets in shops may be overfilled with produce, and, with radiant heat from lighting, the temperature of the food can sometimes be above −10 °C. Temperatures of −18 °C to −23 °C permit only very slow decomposition of the product by the action of its own enzymes, and much of this activity may have been reduced anyway by initial 'blanching' (brief cooking in boiling water). Does deep-freezing kill bacteria? The answer is no, or very rarely. Certainly, it is best to assume that the amount of bacterial contamination will be similar on thawing as on initial freezing. However, the prevention of multiplication of bacteria is an important safety factor. Listeria, for example, probably becomes dangerous only after growing under chilled conditions (i.e. at 0–5 °C), but will not be able to do so in the deep freeze.

If there is a danger with deep-frozen items, it is related to how they are handled after their removal from the freezer. Thawing too soon before final cooking can affect the quality of texture and flavour, and inadequate cooking of thawed produce results in food that still feels cold. It may even contain ice crystals. In such conditions any bacteria present would survive. For these reasons, canned food would generally seem to be marginally preferable to frozen foods, with the proviso that cans must not be kept for long after opening. Of course, some deep-frozen items (e.g. breaded fish) are not available in tins. Specific advice is given in Chapter 9.

Preserved food

The addition of high concentrations of salt and sugar is one traditional method of preserving food because high concentrations create conditions in which food-spoilage organisms and bacteria cannot survive. However, moulds are more resistant to sugar, and the surface of home-made jam and marmalade is sometimes contaminated by them.

The acetic acid in vinegar is also effective as a preservative, so many pickles, chutneys and ketchups should be safe, as long as they are handled according to instructions. In some, however, there is a fairly low concentration of vinegar; while the product should be free from bacteria before opening (a reassuring hiss on opening the top suggests a vacuum associated with a high temperature during assembly), there is a risk of the contamination of these products after opening, so subsequent storage must comply with the label instructions.

Alcohol is a good preservative as long as it is present in high enough concentration. Most spirits contain about 40 per cent ethyl alcohol final concentration by volume (equivalent to about 70 proof), which will inhibit the growth of all micro-organisms. It is therefore safe to keep opened bottles of spirits almost indefinitely. Most fortified wines do not contain quite enough alcohol to prevent the growth of fungi, so they should not be kept open for longer than, say, a week to a month (this advice is necessarily vague because of the variable nature of the products). Beer, cider and wine do not contain adequate alcohol to restrain bacterial growth, but some of these products are so acidic (pH 4–4.5) that only moulds can grow. It follows that these drinks can deteriorate after being open for between twelve and twenty-four hours.

Dried foods

Drying is one of the oldest methods of preserving foods. We are all familiar with dried fruit, raisins and sultanas. In addition, meat and vegetables can be dried, sometimes using natural conditions. However, in practice most food is treated by freeze-drying, which involves the deep freezing of the food, followed by the loss of the ice water into a vacuum and drying. After drying, the food powder (for example, that for making instant coffee, gravy, custard or soup) is placed in an airtight container or packet. We can be confident that, in the absence of water, bacteria in such products will remain in suspended animation and will be unlikely to cause food poisoning – except, of course, if salmonella is present in dried baby milk. If the integrity of the packet or container is breached, moist air may get into the product, with the possibility that bacterial growth will occur. Such products will no longer comprise free-running powder but will be wet and lumpy and should not be used.

However, the real problem with dried food products is that while in the dried state there should be little risk of bacterial growth, as soon as they are made into food for eating the possibilities for bacterial multiplication occur because the initial drying processes at best reduce the numbers of bacteria present slightly, and at worst have no influence at all on numbers. Consider gravy or custard made from dried powder. The temperatures of the reconstituted product may well be no more than 60–70 °C; after an hour or so the bacteria may begin to grow and, if kept warm, the bacteria can rapidly reach dangerous levels. This danger is simply prevented by making up these fluids only in amounts that are required immediately. Left-overs (not expensive) should be discarded.

Although not strictly dried foods, bread and other baked products usually contain insufficient water to permit the ready growth of bacteria. If problems do arise, it is with moulds: we must all be familiar with green areas of discolouration on bread from, for example, the penicillium mould (incidentally the source of the antibiotic penicillin). Many of these moulds are harmless, but there is a possibility that some may be harmful, so mould-contaminated bread products should be discarded.

Pasteurization

The pasteurization of milk involves heating it to 63 °C for thirty minutes or, as is now more usual, heating it to 71.7 °C for at least fifteen seconds, then cooling it to 10 °C. Because of worry about listeria, many American dairies now use a temperature of 76.6 °C for fifteen seconds.

The pasteurization treatment does not kill all micro-organisms, although most of the dangerous species, such as salmonella, *Staphylococci*, *Mycobacteria* and *Brucella*, should be eliminated. Spores – the means by which certain bacteria can enter a dormant phase – may well not be destroyed by pasteurization. At the moment discussions are in progress to make pasteurization of milk a legal requirement before its sale in England and Wales. It has not been possible to purchase unpasteurized milk in Scotland since the early 1980s. During the last few years about twenty deaths have been attributed to drinking unpasteurized milk (green-top). Currently about 5 per cent of milk purchased on the doorstep in West Yorkshire and Lancashire is unpasteurized; enthusiasts for the product claim the flavour is better than that of pasteurized milk. From the safety point of view, we should appreciate that at present bottles of unpasteurized milk do not carry a health warning, and an infection acquired by one individual from unpasteurized milk could spread to another. Such infections could be salmonella, campylobacter or tuberculosis.

Irradiation

Irradiation, which is the subjection of objects to waves and particles generated by a radioactive source, is able to kill all living organisms, including bacteria in food. At the moment this technique is not permitted in the UK but it is now under discussion and may be introduced in the future. The first point to make is that food treated with irradiation is not radioactive – that is, the rays cannot be passed from the food to the consumer. It is also highly likely – but not absolutely certain – that such treatment does not leave any dangerous chemicals in the food. We still have some slight reservations about safety here because there is a possibility that small amounts of active harmful chemicals may be found that have not so far been identified. Although this risk would seem small, there are other problems associated with irradiation.

- While the process may destroy all the actual whole bacteria, it may not remove all the toxins that food-poisoning bacteria may have released into the product.
- It is difficult to be certain that every single item has been adequately treated.
- Contamination of the food may occur after irradiation, particularly if the packaging is flimsy.
- Natural enzymes causing the disintegration of the food may survive after irradiation in certain foods.
- The public may be lulled into a sense of false security about the quality of the food as a whole, and hygiene

standards may drop all along the line, from producer and retailer to the home, with added risks.

- There is genuine public concern that we should be endeavouring to reduce the number and scale of emitters of radiation, in order to reduce the risks to plant workers and the local community, possible access by terrorists and the apparently insoluble problem of disposal of radioactive waste.

Despite these reservations, it is likely that many people have already eaten food treated by irradiation. The reason for this is that irradiation of certain foods is already permissible in certain countries. If you have been surprised by the good condition of, say, strawberries bought in the winter, they may have been irradiated before being imported from overseas! This treatment may well be reasonable, but its extension to other foods needs to be thought through very carefully.

3
Food poisoning: detection and spread

Let's start by seeing how a typical episode of food
poisoning occurs, how it is reported and then how it is
tracked down to a particular food. The following incident happened in 1988; only the names have been
altered. The likely cause of this food poisoning was
that a cook was harbouring salmonella in his intestines
and, as a result of bad personal hygiene, transferred it
to a dish of beef and mushrooms that was then kept
warm for too long.

Mrs Wiggins was a part-time secretary for a company
that manufactured kitchen fittings. One Monday an
unusual amount of extra work forced her to work later
than usual into the afternoon. This meant there was
insufficient time for the preparation of the family's usual
early-evening meal, which that day was to have been
roast chicken and vegetables. So Mrs Wiggins called in
at a Chinese take-away, the Happy Hour, arriving home
shortly afterwards, at 5.30 p.m., with beef and mushrooms, chicken with prawn chop suey, sweet and sour
pork and egg-fried rice. These were warmed up at 6.00
p.m., and together with freshly fried prawn crackers,
constituted the meal which the family sat down to eat
at about 6.15 or 6.30 p.m. All was well until late
morning on the next day, Tuesday, when Mr and Mrs
Wiggins and one of their two sons developed frequent

diarrhoea, suffered from colicky tummy aches and felt shivery and hot in turns. In addition, Mrs Wiggins had vomited up her breakfast. By that afternoon all three of the affected members of the family had returned home and were convinced they had food poisoning; they laid the blame on the Chinese take-away. They telephoned their group practice surgery, and the doctor arrived at 3.30 p.m. with specimen containers for samples of faeces to be sent to the microbiology laboratory. The doctor agreed that food poisoning was likely and made two immediate decisions. First, he told the Wiggins family to prevent the dustbin containing the left-overs from last night's meal from being emptied, and he telephoned his medical colleague at the city's Environmental Health Department to alert him to the possibility that food poisoning may have been caused by the Happy Hour take-away.

The three members of the Wiggins family were examined by the doctor, who found them to be fairly ill and extremely worried. Because none of the patients had recently suffered from any other serious illness and all could drink fluids, the doctor decided that they were well enough to be treated at home. However, he explained that if their condition became worse and they could not swallow fluids, admission to hospital might be needed. He prescribed immodium tablets to help stop the diarrhoea and told them to stay in bed and to drink plenty of fluids, preferably water or fruit juices. If they could manage these, they could change over to milky products and then solid food when possible. Fortunately, Mrs Wiggins's mother was able to look after them. At this stage it was not possible to be certain which type of food poisoning the family was experiencing, but salmonella, *Bacillus cereus* or *Clostridium perfringens* were possible. The laboratory should be able to give an answer in a day or two. Fortunately, the specimens from the three patients arrived at the laboratory by 5.00 p.m. that day, and the scientist worked late in view of the possible importance of these cases. (It is always essential to find out exactly the cause of food poisoning, not just for the sake of the treatment of the people known to be affected, but also to prevent a large number of other people from becoming ill.)

By 6.15 p.m. that evening the specimens had been studied under the microscope and applied to the surface of a number of gels containing nutrients and chemicals that would enable each of the various food-poisoning bacteria to grow; they had also been put into fluids that enable small numbers of bacteria to be concentrated after growing. The fluids and gels were then put into warm incubators at 37 °C and 41 °C. Under the microscope the bacteria seen in each specimen did not give any clues as to the cause of the food poisoning. This was not unusual because the shape and size of food-poisoning bacteria are often similar to those of harmless bacteria that may be present in the intestines. The fluids and gels needed to be incubated overnight, for between fourteen and eighteen hours at least, before sufficient growth of the bacteria had occurred for their identification to begin. The scientist could do no more at that point.

Meanwhile the Environmental Health Department was busy. One of its officers visited the Wigginses' home and, as carefully as possible, transferred the remains of the previous evening's meal to sterile containers, avoiding touching the food himself or making contact with other debris in the bin. Details of this procedure, including the time, were recorded. He then took the food samples to the Public Health Laboratory, which is expert at identifying the bacteria that cause food poisoning. The work in the laboratory was completed by 7 p.m., and preliminary results were to be available the next day.

The other action taken by the Environmental Health Department was to send two officers to visit the Happy Hour take-away. At this stage there was no proof at all that the presumed food poisoning was due to food supplied by this source – indeed, the three patients might have become ill by breathing in, or swallowing, a virus that can cause similar problems. But if there are dangerous practices in any catering establishment, environmental health officers have a responsibility to prevent other customers from becoming ill. When three patients are reported to be suffering from food poisoning it is never possible to tell if these will be the only three or if a large number of cases will occur subsequently. The environmental health officers proceeded discreetly and removed samples of most suspect food ready for sale. The owner of the take-away insisted that batches of food were made ready for purchase at frequent intervals and that although the shop was open from 11 a.m. to 11 p.m., no food was kept warm for longer than two hours. The officers found the general level of hygiene reasonable, but they did notice that the cooks were wearing untidy, frayed clothes and overalls and that two had long, uncovered hair. Many cigarette stubs were seen in ashtrays. The food samples were then taken to the Public Health Laboratory, and again times and details were accurately recorded.

The next day provided four pieces of information. First, the three patients felt less ill; the pain and diarrhoea had eased, and a feeling of exhaustion was now the main symptom. Then the local laboratory came up with potentially important findings. From each of the specimens that had been put on one type of gel nearly transparent, shiny blobs of bacterial growth had appeared, and these could well be a type of salmonella, although it might be two or more days before definite proof could be obtained. Next, in the Public Health Laboratory similar results were obtained from the remnants of food in the Wigginses' dustbin and also, very important, from one of the samples removed from the Happy Hour take-away. This sample was from the beef and mushrooms. The other foods were negative. The final piece of information on Wednesday was that eleven other people who had purchased food from the take-away were ill with probable food poisoning. By midday on Wednesday the Environmental Health Department had requested that the shop suspend sales and hold all its food stock for analysis. The owner complied with this – if he had not, the Environmental Health Department could have sought an order from the magistrates' court, and the publicity might have been damaging to the Happy Hour.

During the next few days the total number of people affected rose to thirty, though, fortunately, none was sufficiently ill to require admission to hospital. By Friday – four days after the incident began – further testing of the bacteria had shown that the type was *Salmonella enteritidis*. (This is the type often associated with eggs.) Because there is more than one subtype of *Salmonella enteritidis*, the bacteria were sent to

Colindale, London, where the identification of the sub-type was to be made. By the following Wednesday the bacteria had been identified accurately as *Salmonella enteritidis*, type 4.

Meanwhile investigations were proceeding into how a salmonella normally found in eggs and poultry was contaminating the beef and mushrooms. The raw ingredients used for this dish were all tested and found not to contain salmonella. Tests on the cooking equipment were also negative, but the container that held this dish before sale was definitely contaminated by salmonella. It is important to understand that when a largeish number of otherwise healthy people develop food poisoning simultaneously the number of bacteria present in the food is likely to be high. Salmonella would probably have been present in large numbers in the beef and mushroom dish; if so, the bacteria must have been growing in the finished food for some hours, since it appeared to be absent from the raw ingredients. On the day that the Wiggins family became ill, the take-away had opened at 11 a.m.; the owner, as we have seen, claimed that the meals were made up at intervals of two hours or less. All thirty sufferers had bought their food in the late afternoon. Could the suspect food have been made up much earlier, become contaminated and been kept warm for six hours? Or was there another explanation? A possible source of the bacteria could be one of the cooks. Early on in the investigation specimens from all the staff at the Happy Hour were examined for salmonella. While none had reported recent diarrhoea, the specimen from one cook did indeed contain *Salmonella enteritidis*, later to be identified as type 4. The likely events are therefore as follows. The cook prepared the beef and mushrooms. The raw ingredients were safe, but salmonella on his fingers from bad personal hygiene contaminated the food, which was then kept warm for too long, allowing the bacteria to multiply sufficiently to cause food poisoning. (Regrettably, a substantial number of people must now be harbouring *Salmonella enteritidis*, including people involved in food preparation, as a result of eating contaminated eggs and poultry over the last few years.)

The reason why this incident has been described in such detail is to show that the tracking down of a food-poisoning outbreak involves a great deal of hard work and is both costly and time-consuming. While the investigation was successful in this instance, often it is not. Everything went well here. The patients contacted their doctor in time for specimens to be tested that day; the Environmental Health Department was alerted the same day; and, most important, the salmonella was found in the remains of the food. A great deal of the uncertainty over the danger of salmonella from eggs is related to the fact that an egg yolk will often be eaten entirely; there are no left-overs that can be tested. Some institutions and hospitals voluntarily keep samples of food from all their meals for four days in case food poisoning needs to be traced, but many restaurants and other food outlets do not, and this measure cannot be enforced.

GUESSING AT THE REAL INCIDENCE OF FOOD POISONING

The official food-poisoning figures in the UK are obtained from the reports of laboratories each time a food-poisoning bacterium is found. The numbers go to a central statistical agency run by the government with the long-winded title of the Public Health Laboratory Service Communicable Disease Surveillance Centre. There are many reasons why the official number of food-poisoning cases represents only a small fraction of the real number. First, in this country our overall approach to food poisoning tends to be passive; that is, we react to information given, rather than going into hospitals, institutions and people's homes to assess actively how many people suffer from food poisoning. In the USA there is a more positive attitude, and certainly some of their approaches are more successful than ours. Next, patients with food poisoning may not go to their doctor, particularly if they suspect the food poisoning was their own fault. Sometimes the disease appears familiar (regrettably!) or is not too severe. Even if a patient visits his doctor, the doctor may not be inclined to trouble hard-pressed laboratories to test specimens that they can hardly afford to examine. At present most laboratories that do work for general practitioners are paid out of hospital funds. Other reasons for the inaccurate reporting of food-poisoning cases are that a patient may be too shy to offer faeces for testing and that a laboratory may forget to report the presence of the bacteria. As the law stands at present, the onus is on the attending doctor, not the laboratory, to notify food poisoning if it is due to certain bacteria such as salmonella. All these factors add up to the likelihood that the number of reported cases of food poisoning does not reflect the real incidence of food poisoning in the UK.

While we do not know the true figures, it is certain that the official numbers understate the problem, although it is not clear by how much. Some American specialists believe that only one in 100 cases are notified, so they multiply by 100 to convert the reported cases to the level believed to indicate the real figures. One of the problems here is the definition of food poisoning. Does a slight tummy pain lasting a few minutes, with one episode of diarrhoea, amount to food poisoning? When does a change in bowel habit indicate simply a result of changing diet? When is diarrhoea due to allergy to certain foods or to food poisoning? Do some patients accept a degree of discomfort that cannot be tolerated by others? We cannot simply diagnose food poisoning by growing the bacteria in question from faeces, since most food-poisoning bacteria are commonly found in the environment, and between 1 and 5 per cent of the population may be carrying salmonella in their intestines without suffering from it.

The American multiplier of 100 may well be appropriate to cover all possible cases, including those that are of a fairly minor nature. In the UK most experts prefer a multiplier of 10, although no one would dispute that it should perhaps be 5 or 20. (A multiplier of 10 means that if 10,000 reports of food poisoning are made in a year, we believe that 100,000 have occurred.)

While we remain uncertain about the total number of annual food-poisoning cases, the available figures provide more precise information about trends. Since 1983, for example, our laboratory methods of identifying salmonella have not changed; nor have the general reporting procedures and involvement of doctors and Environmental Health Departments. We can assume that the fraction of the real cases of food poisoning that are reported each year remains approximately constant.

When looking at the events in the UK over the last few years I propose, therefore, to arrive at the real figures by multiplying each annual reported number by 10.

THE FOOD-POISONING EPIDEMIC IN THE UK

The number of salmonella cases in England, Wales and Northern Ireland was about 111,000–140,000 between 1980 and 1985. Since 1985 each year has seen a rise; about 250,000 cases occurred in 1988. In the first two months of 1989 the numbers were up by 17 per cent on the same period in 1988. This increase is quite remarkable: *Salmonella enteritidis* is mainly responsible and is caught predominantly from eggs. We estimate that in 1989 egg eating is down by about 20 per cent on 1988, so the recent increase in *Salmonella enteritidis* is very disturbing.

Other food-poisoning cases are also on the increase. Campylobacter has jumped from about 200,000 cases annually in 1985 to nearly 300,000 in 1988. Listeriosis has also increased about threefold in this period. (Details of the incidence of this disease will be given in Chapter 5.)

Overall, the number of people suffering from food poisoning is now around 750,000 annually, compared with about half this number in 1983. The figures for 1989 are the worst ever. The unnecessary loss of about 300 lives annually, the suffering from the illness, absenteeism from work and the costs are adversely affecting all of us.

4
The nasty poisons

In this chapter food poisoning due to *Clostridium botulinum*, *Clostridium perfringens* and *Staphylococcus aureus* will be explained. None of these has been much in the news recently, but one in particular – that caused by *Clostridium botulinum* – could return unless the catering industry addresses the problem. All three of these bacteria have in common the formation of potent poisons that escape from them into the food where they have been growing. The diseases they cause are due to the poisons rather than to the bacteria themselves. The effects can often be severe and rapid and may damage the brain.

BOTULISM

The disease botulism is named after the Latin word *botulus*, meaning a sausage. Sausages and other processed meats have been shown to cause botulism, although the most common source of the disease over the years has been canned vegetables that have not been heated adequately. However, the sausage does help us to understand how the bacterium *Clostridium botulinum* causes food poisoning. This bacterium is extremely tough and survives heat and drying by changing itself into small hard spheres, or spores. These remain inactive and do not produce the poison unless conditions are right for them to change back into growing bacteria. The three conditions needed for this are warmth, moisture and nutrients, and an atmosphere that contains no oxygen.

Oxygen is, course, essential for man, but some bacteria, such as *Clostridium botulinum*, are killed by it. Such bacteria are described as 'anaerobic'. To return to the sausage: if it is not refrigerated adequately, warmth, moisture and nutrients will be present, and in the centre there may be an absence of oxygen. This can occur because chemicals such as hydrogen and sulphur remove any oxygen present in the centre of the sausage through various reactions.

The bacterium *Clostridium botulinum* is widely found in the world, sometimes in its actively growing long, or 'bacillary', form but usually as tough spores, waiting for their chance to start growing when conditions are just right. It has been found in soil, sludges, sediments, some animal droppings, sea water and – most important – on fish. It has been estimated that about 5 per cent of all soil samples contain *Clostridium botulinum*. This is a good example of food poisoning that frequently results from a commonly distributed bacterium that becomes dangerous only after growing under particular conditions that just happen to occur. As far as we are aware, there has been no case of botulism in the UK for over ten years. Many of our vegetables are still contaminated with this bacterium, so we have learnt how to reduce its dangers.

The poisons of *Clostridium botulinum* are frightening. There are at least eight similar toxins, referred to simply as A, B, C and so on. Each is a large protein consisting of about 1,500 of the amino-acid subunits, or building blocks, of the protein. But why is a protein dangerous? Do we not eat proteins every day? Moreover, do we not *have* to eat proteins, the enzymes in our intestines splitting them up to release the component amino-acids? It is these that are absorbed and used by the body for essential purposes. The answer to all these questions is yes. But, unfortunately, the protein toxins of *Clostridium botulinum* are almost completely immune to the effects of digestive juices, so they are not split up into harmless small pieces but are absorbed more or less intact (exactly how is something of a mystery and difficult to experiment on). After food contaminated with the growing *Clostridium botulinum* has been eaten the toxin moves through the wall of the gut into small channels, known as lymphatics, that convey it to the blood stream. Once in the blood stream, it is conveyed within minutes all around the body. The delay of between twelve and twenty-four hours between eating contaminated food and becoming very ill is probably the result of the time needed to get the toxin through the intestine into the blood. The toxin does its damage by interfering with one of the most vital pathways in the body – the junction between the nerves and the muscles. Our muscles work only as a result of being stimulated by messages from the nerves, known as nervous impulses. The botulinum toxin disrupts this process completely. The toxin does its damage by preventing the nervous impulse from passing from the nerve to the muscle. It is so potent that it is possible that only one molecule of it is needed to do the damage at each junction between the nerve and the muscle.

Estimates of the amounts of toxin needed to kill a person vary from about a millionth of a gram to a hundred millionth. If the latter figure is correct, 1 gram, or a twenty-eighth of 1 ounce – perhaps the weight of a bean – could kill the entire population of the UK. No wonder the possible use of botulinum toxin in warfare or for criminal purposes has always been a popular fictional scare. This is certainly the most potent of all known poisons, in food or otherwise. There appears to be no sensible explanation of why a common soil bacterium should produce such a dangerous poison. Surely its production must be an unfortunate accident? We should be thankful that the tens of thousands of other soil bacteria do not produce poisons like this.

Fortunately, the disease caused by *Clostridium botulinum* has become rare, and we have learned, often the hard way, how to control it. Much of our information about this and other food-poisoning bacteria comes from the USA. It was home-canned food in the USA in the early part of this century that caused most problems, although canned food purchased from shops was also sometimes to blame. Indeed, the last cases of botulism in the UK were associated with a standard supermarket product. Vegetables have been responsible for more cases than meat, presumably because of the presence of soil contamination that contains the growing bacteria or, more important, the spores. Canned fruit has also been responsible for botulism. One of the types of *Clostridium botulinum*, type E, is particularly associated with fish, including salmon, and this has caused problems in some vacuum-packed fish. In order for botulism to occur, the food has to be contaminated with the bacteria, either as the tough spores in the first place or as the growing bacteria that can be produced from spores. The next requirement, if botulism is to occur, is that the processing must fail to eliminate all the spores. The required temperatures for their elimination during canning are now known and depend partly on the acidity of the food. Today the chief question concerns the risks of accidents when adequate temperatures are not reached for long enough. (Previously, many of the temperatures reached were not high enough.) Survival of the spore itself will not cause botulism: the spores do not produce toxin. The danger lies in the fact that the can may be stored under conditions that permit the spores to be converted to the growing bacteria. For this to happen, we have seen that adequate warmth, moisture and nutrients, and the absence of oxygen, are needed. However, conditions in some cans may be too acidic for growth. So even if spores are found in some cans, it is by no means inevitable that botulism will result, but it is absolutely essential that our food-preparation procedures eliminate these risks.

To give an idea of the number of cases of botulism at its height, we know that between 1899 and 1969, 1,696 people were affected in the USA; there were 959 deaths. Figures in the UK for the equivalent period were lower. One of the best-known instances of botulism occurred in 1922 at Loch Maree, near Gairloch, in Scotland. Eight visitors who had been staying at a local hotel decided to make a fishing trip to the loch on 14 August. Their snacks included sandwiches filled with duck paste (presumably from a tin). The first member became ill at 3 a.m. the next morning, and during the subsequent week all eight people died of botulism. Some of the duck paste was available for examination, as was one of the sandwiches. From both samples the bacterium itself and the toxin were identified. (One of the problems with botulism is the food contaminated with it and with the poison may not taste particularly abnormal.)

Between this incident and 1978 about nine cases of botulism occurred in the UK; two people acquired it as a result of eating pickled fish from Mauritius. It was 1978 that saw our last reported outbreak of botulism. A detailed description of this will indicate the effect of the toxin on certain muscles.

Four friends, aged between 64 and 75, met for afternoon tea. Two were men, two women. Tinned Alaskan salmon and fruit and cream were eaten at about 5.00 p.m. The food tasted as expected. The illness in all four was similar. Between nine and eleven hours later – between 2 and 4 a.m. the following morning – the first unpleasant sensation was nausea, followed by vomiting. Each patient also complained of a dry mouth. Dizziness and blurred or double vision followed. By 7 a.m. all the patients had been admitted to hospital. Each showed paralysis of most of the limb muscles and had extreme difficulty in speaking and swallowing. Each was now beginning to suffer difficulty with breathing as a result of paralysis of the muscles around the chest and of the diaphragm under the lungs. Shortly after admission all were placed on life-support machines, mainly to ensure that their breathing was maintained artificially. (One sinister aspect of this disease is that the harmful effects of botulism are confined to the junction between nerves and muscles. The nerves that enable us to feel and see and think are not affected. So while patients are paralysed, their level of consciousness and their senses are nearly normal. For this reason, some sedation is given.)

Unfortunately, once the toxin has done its damage, it

is very difficult to repair, and during the subsequent weeks two of the patients died. Two recovered nearly completely. In view of the severity of this infection, I believe the medical teams should be congratulated profoundly for the two survivors.

The bacteriological investigations revealed that the toxin *Clostridium botulinum*, type E, was present in the blood of all four patients. (Remember that this is the toxin type associated with fish.) The salmon tin was recovered, and the first staining tests showed that structures that looked like spores and the growing bacteria were present. Subsequently, *Clostridium botulinum*, type E, was grown, and the toxin was found in the salmon itself. At the time there was speculation that the *Clostridium* bacteria had gained entry to the tin through a small defect in the tin or through a rust hole. There was no evidence of this, a more likely explanation being that the *Clostridium* was in the raw salmon and that, by some accident, the temperature during canning had not been sufficiently high. It was reassuring that 14,000 other tins were then tested and found not to contain any such contamination.

A somewhat more recent case from the USA illustrates other points. The story is adapted from the American reports, which, oddly, do not tell us whether the patient recovered.

On 3 August 1982, a 56-year-old woman living in Los Angeles County, California, became ill, complaining of double vision, weakness of her arms and legs, difficulty in catching her breath and pains in her chest. Soon after being admitted to hospital, her breathing stopped altogether. Fortunately, the emergency team was near; a tube was passed into her windpipe, and she was placed on an artificial respirator. In previous years she had had a number of illnesses, including diabetes. While in hospital over the next day or so, she developed pneumonia and a high fever, thought to be the result of bacteria in her lungs. A possible cause of her general paralysis was thought to be botulism, so her food history was explored.

The patient lived with her husband and grown-up son, who were both in the habit of preparing meals for her, aware of her requirements as a diabetic. Some days before the onset of her illness her son had baked a frozen meat pie for forty to forty-five minutes in the oven. Just as he was about to serve the meat pie, his father came home with some freshly cooked hamburgers, just bought from a take-away restaurant. The meat pie was put to one side on an unrefrigerated shelf (recall: the month was August and the family lived in California – it was presumably hot). Two and a half days later the son came home and found that his mother had eaten the pie without reheating it. Investigations showed that the pie contained the toxin produced by *Clostridium botulinum*, type A; the same substance was present in the patient's blood.

We can work out what went wrong. The initial baking of the pie may have killed off most of the bacteria except the spores produced by the *Clostridium botulinum* bacteria. The baking would also have boiled off any oxygen gas in the centre of the pie. The pie, instead of being eaten, was kept under warm conditions, ideal for the conversion of the surviving spores to the growing forms of the bacterium. Finally, in the absence of any reheating, all the toxin would have survived intact. A disaster.

We have not considered so far whether the cooking or reheating of a product can be relied on to decompose any toxin that may have been formed during storage of the food. The speed with which heating deactivates these toxins depends on three factors: the temperature, the length of time that the food is subjected to heat and the nature of the food. In addition the various toxins of *Clostridium botulinum* vary in their resistance to heat. In general, the toxins are fairly resistant to heat. Types A and B need to be heated to 80 °C for up to ten minutes; at the other extreme, type E should be destroyed after five minutes at 60 °C.

The difficulty of reheating food to high temperatures comes as a surprise to many people. We shall be considering this in more detail in Part II. As far as botulism is concerned, we cannot rely on reheating to destroy any toxins. Instead we must ensure that our method of food production is such that it will not permit the formation of these poisons with their hideous effects on us. And there should be a margin of safety.

We have learned how to prevent botulism through experience – the hard way. We now understand that a bacterium that is commonly found in the environment can, under certain conditions that have to be just right, produce the most potent human poison ever found. Let us hope botulism is a disease of the past. Incredibly, a current new catering technique is now being introduced that could well cause botulism once more. This technique is described as *sous vide*.

Sous vide

Sous vide is French for 'under a vacuum'. The idea of this technique is for restaurants, canteens or even homes to have available whole or part meals that require only reheating.

The procedure begins with the pasteurization of assembled whole meals or components. This initial heat treatment does not destroy the spores of bacteria — possibly it does not destroy listeria. The food is cooled rapidly and then enclosed in a packet; air is removed and replaced typically by nitrogen and carbon dioxide. The atmosphere in the pack is therefore anaerobic (i.e. no oxygen is present), so conditions are ideal for the growth of any spores of *Clostridium botulinum* that might have survived the first cooking. The packs are stored under refrigerated conditions for, say, three to six weeks and reheated when required, frequently in microwave ovens. This would seem to be a possible recipe for disaster, not just in the view of the author of this book but in the eyes of many people involved with food safety. The reasons for the dangers are as follows. First, we all know that it is rarely possible to control refrigerator temperatures as closely as we would like. Gauges can be inaccurate; doors can be left open; lighting can warm up products through radiant heat; and even an ideal range of temperature of 0–5 °C is not sufficient to stop the growth of *Clostridium botulinum*, type E, which can multiply and therefore produce its toxin at a temperature as low as 3.3 °C. The other reason is that the reheating of the product may well not be sufficient to destroy these toxins. Microwaves are notorious for their 'cold spots' — this issue will be considered in Part II. Also to be considered will be the extraordinary legislation that permits the development of this dangerous type of catering.

CLOSTRIDIUM PERFRINGENS

Food poisoning caused by *Clostridium perfringens* is much less severe than that caused by *Clostridium botulinum*, but is more common and entirely preventable. *Clostridium perfringens* spores are resistant to most ordinary cooking temperatures and, if present in, say, a large stew in a saucepan that is allowed to cool only slowly or kept warm overnight in a kitchen, can give rise to the growing forms of the bacteria that may produce the toxin. In addition the toxin can be produced inside a patient's intestines if a large number of bacteria are eaten. The toxin is known as an enterotoxin: it damages the intestines, which results in a moderately severe diarrhoea between twelve and eighteen hours after the contaminated food has been eaten.

Most healthy people carry small numbers of *Clostridium perfringens* in their intestines; it is also found widely in the environment and in other animals. Prevention of food poisoning from the bacteria is simply achieved by not providing the right conditions for it to multiply in foods such as stews. This means that such foods must not be kept at temperatures of, say, 30–50 °C for longer than one and a half hours. Further details are discussed in Part II.

STAPHYLOCOCCAL FOOD POISONING

Staphylococci are small, rounded bacteria distributed very widely in the human body, particularly in the skin and in the nose. One type of staphylococcus, *Staphylococcus aureus*, produces a large variety of enzymes, proteins and toxins related to many diseases such as infections of bones, boils, styes and abscesses. Like the toxins of the *Clostridium*, these products escape from the bacterium as it grows. A few subtypes of *Staphylococcus aureus* produce a toxin that causes food poisoning. If these bacteria get into certain foods that are kept warm for several hours, the bacteria can multiply in large numbers, and, as they increase, so the toxin is released into the food. The foods most likely to be affected are meats (particularly chicken), creams, custards and baked products containing fillings. The toxin produced is usually described as an enterotoxin, although it is rapidly absorbed from the stomach after the food is eaten. It then appears to track up the nerves from the stomach to the brain, where its effect is to cause vomiting, sometimes accompanied by the appearance of blood. This can be quite distressing. Usually the vomiting begins between thirty minutes and three hours after eating the contaminated food. Because the toxin is resistant to normal cooking, the reheating of contaminated food will not make dangerous food safe. As with *Clostridium perfringens*, this type of food poisoning is preventable by not letting food stand at warm temperatures.

5
Listeriosis – the new food poisoning

The bacterium that causes the disease listeriosis is *Listeria monocytogenes* and was named after the famous nineteenth-century surgeon Lord Lister, who pioneered antisepsis to prevent infections after surgery. The disease was first found in a rabbit in 1926, then in a human adult in 1929 and in a baby in 1936. For over fifty years since its detection listeria has been thought to be passed to man by animals, although exactly how has remained a mystery. Certainly, the disease can occur in a number of animals. During the last few years it has caused illness principally in sheep and, to a lesser extent, in cattle and other animals, although infection in poultry seems rare. Currently every year several hundreds of reports of listeriosis are made by veterinary surgeons looking after sheep and cattle. The effect of the disease on these animals can be to cause miscarriages or distressing brain damage, sometimes accompanied by blindness, paralysis of certain muscles and a characteristic unsteady walk, often allied with a tendency for the animal to wander in circles. In the case of sheep, in which the disease is best understood, it occurs mainly in the cold winter and early spring months and is thought to be related to silage that may be contaminated with droppings or soil from molehills. Interestingly, the human disease is also associated with food that has been stored at cold temperatures. The number of sheep and cattle inflicted with listeriosis has increased over the last five years, but there is little reason to blame these animals for human infection.

Since the early reports of listeriosis in people in the 1920s and 1930s, for more than fifty years we did not really understand how the disease infected us. During this time a number of outbreaks affecting large numbers of people occurred; although food and milk were thought to be the possible sources, no proof had been obtained.

However, in 1981 results of some careful work in the eastern provinces of Canada, with help from American experts, established that coleslaw was the cause of many cases of listeriosis. The people involved were thirty-four pregnant women and seven other adults. Of the pregnant women who were infected each had had an illness with fever, to be followed by miscarriage in five cases, stillbirth (later in pregnancy) in four, the live birth of a seriously ill baby in twenty-three and the live birth of a well baby in only two. Seven babies born alive later died. This means that among the babies of the thirty-four pregnant women suffering from listeriosis sixteen died before or after birth. Of the seven other adults who suffered, six had meningitis and two died. Interestingly, on this occasion none of the adults had abnormalities in their immune system. The patients' listeria was a particular type, known as 4b, and the same bacterium was found in the uneaten coleslaw. The coleslaw had been made from radishes, cabbages and carrots from a number of farms. One farmer who grew cabbages also kept a flock of sheep. Two of these sheep had died in 1979 and early 1981 from listeriosis.

It seems that the cabbage was grown in fields fertilized by rotted and raw manure from the flock of sheep. After being harvested during each October, the cabbages were stored over winter in a large cold shed.

We can now explain fully how the coleslaw became contaminated with listeria. The sheep manure contaminated the soil and growing cabbage with the bacteria, at first in small numbers but increasingly during the storage of the cabbage. When mayonnaise or dressing was added to the still raw vegetables the extra nutrients permitted the listeria to multiply during its storage either in the shops or in the home. The fact that seven previously well people suffered from the disease suggests that very large numbers of bacteria were present.

Now that the link between food and listeriosis has been established in one major outbreak, we can review other outbreaks and draw similar conclusions. The outbreaks in 1955–81 were all probably due to contaminated food. Since 1981 a number of further outbreaks have occurred, and there is good evidence that certain foods were responsible.

The outbreak in Massachusetts in 1983 is interesting in that pasteurization of milk should have destroyed any listeria present. Listeria is fairly resistant to heat, and it is possible that the bacteria did, in fact, survive the pasteurization temperature of 71.6 °C held for fifteen seconds. Alternatively, the Massachusetts outbreak could have been due to contamination of the milk after pasteurization. In this connection the Swiss cheese outbreak was probably due to contamination of the cheese after manufacture from pasteurized milk.

Incidence of Listeriosis 1955–81

Place, country	Date	Number of infected patients
Prague, Czechoslovakia	1955	41
Bremen, West Germany	1960–61	61
Bremen, West Germany	1963	20
Halle, East Germany	1966	279
Auckland, New Zealand	1969	20
Greenville, USA	1975	6
Anjou, France	1976	162
Perth, Australia	1978	4
Perth, Australia	1979	6
Auckland, New Zealand	1980	21
Carlisle, UK	1981	11

Outbreaks of Listeriosis 1983–7

Place, country	Date	Number and details of infected patients	Food involved
Massachusetts, USA	1983	49 cases, 14 deaths	Pasteurized milk
California, USA	1985	142 cases, 48 deaths	Mexican-type soft cheese
Switzerland	1983–7	122 cases, 62 pregnant women, 31 deaths	Vacherin cheese

THE LOS ANGELES OUTBREAK

This has been the largest properly documented outbreak of food-borne listeriosis. A total of 142 cases of listeriosis occurred between January and August 1985. Of these ninety-three were pregnant women (oddly, for statistical purposes mothers carrying babies count as one case), and forty-nine were non-pregnant adults. None of the pregnant women died, but thirty babies died altogether, ten around birth and twenty before being born. Most of the infected adults had illnesses that made them vulnerable to the infection. Only one patient appeared to have no predisposing disease or condition.

In tracking down the source of the infection the most striking finding was that nearly all the patients were of Latin American or Hispanic origin. It became clear that Mexican-style soft cheese was very popular among these people. Indeed, there was a close correlation

Conditions that Predispose Patients to Listeriosis

Conditions/drugs/age	Number of patients
Cancer	3
Steroid drugs	12
Diabetes, renal disease, heart failure, alcoholic cirrhosis	23
Over 65 years of age	5
AIDS	3
Following childbirth	2
TOTAL	48

between listeriosis and eating just one type of this cheese. Laboratory studies did indeed find that the same listeria that was recovered from the patients was in the cheese and also in the factory. By June 1985 all samples of the cheese were recalled from the shops, and the factory was closed. It was felt likely that the *Listeria monocytogenes* had been introduced through contamination of the cheese with unpasteurized milk.

Since that time two of the directors of the company have served prison sentences, and claims for damages are proceeding through the courts. As a result of this incidence, new legislation and controls have been implemented.

LISTERIOSIS IN THE UK

So far no big listeriosis epidemic has occurred in the UK; rather, we have seen a progressive increase in reported cases from around twenty or thirty per year twenty years ago to about 300 in 1988. Most of the cases have been one-offs. Because our reporting system probably misses many cases, we estimate the real number of cases as about 800–900, with 200 or so deaths every year. With salmonella a multiplication factor of 10 is often used; because listeriosis is usually more serious, rather fewer cases will be missed – hence the multiplier used is 3. It is true that only four cases (two in Leeds) have formally been proved to have come from food, but since 1986 there is no explanation other than food for any of the other cases that have occurred, mainly in towns. Few patients have stated recent contact with farm animals. All the cases in the world with a proven source other than food probably add up to less than ten. One patient became ill after breathing in the listeria bacterium; a few poultry workers developed sore eyes through direct contact; and a few veterinary surgeons have acquired infected cuts.

Recent publicity on television and the papers demonstrate that in the UK we now appreciate that food is the main source. However, at the time of writing, in March 1989, no worthwhile response to control the disease has come from the government, and the food industry has done little to prevent the sale of food contaminated with listeria.

Food-borne listeriosis is not unique as a new infection. Campylobacter, another cause of food poisoning (see Chapter 7), AIDS and Legionnaire's Disease were also unknown twenty years ago. The scale of the problem of *Salmonella enteritidis* (see Chapter 6) and bovine spongiform encephalopathy (BSE: see Chapter 15) are new. The number and variety of micro-organisms that are capable of harming us seem endless, and the new diseases must reflect changes in the way we live and eat.

From the point of view of making our food safe, listeriosis is the greatest problem at present, and it will not be eliminated by the application of controls such as the use of refrigeration, which has already been developed successfully for the control of certain other food-borne pathogens. Unfortunately, refrigeration, so essential to reduce the risk of salmonella and botulism, may actually encourage listeriosis.

THE NATURE OF THE DISEASE

Some of the ways in which *Listeria monocytogenes* causes disease have been publicized recently, usually fairly accurately. About one third of reported cases involve pregnant women who develop a moderately severe, flu-like illness with temperatures of 38–39 °C lasting from several days to two weeks or more. As far as is known, the pregnant woman is not at risk from death, but the baby is at risk from either miscarriage or stillbirth. Sometimes the baby can be treated after birth, although brain damage can ensue, a tragedy of immense proportions. In the elderly and in patients who are vulnerable the disease manifests itself as blood poisoning, sometimes accompanied by meningitis. In these patients the fever is as high as 40 °C, and the patient may be confused. Oddly, patients with AIDS rarely acquire listeriosis. This is thought to be unusual because of the depressed immunity in patients with AIDS; that is, AIDS patients might be thought to be particularly vulnerable to listeriosis. In all infected patients the risk of dying is about 25–30 per cent. Although pregnant women do not succumb, the risk of the baby's death is not known because we do not know how many of the 100,000 miscarriages or so occurring each year in the UK are due to listeriosis.

It is also not known how effective antibiotics are in treating the disease. Treatment is difficult because the bacterium attacks and resides inside human cells that protect it from some antibiotics. A few otherwise healthy individuals develop listeriosis, and there is a possibility that this is increasing, probably because of the ingestion of very high numbers of bacteria from refrigerated coleslaw or soft cheeses. In the USA, where an active surveillance system is used (that is, the full number of cases are identified), a recent estimate is an annual incidence of 1,600 cases (counting mothers and babies as one) and 400–450 deaths.

THE CAUSE OF LISTERIOSIS

Listeria monocytogenes is widely found in our environment and a small percentage of healthy people can harbour it, usually in small numbers. Why, then, does this illness occur? There are two facts that may account for it. One is that in the 1,000 or so instances of listeriosis that have been shown to come from food, almost all the people who became ill did so after eating food that had been kept refrigerated – usually until just before it had been eaten. Secondly, the bacterium produces large amounts of its toxin, known as listeriolysin, while it is growing at low temperatures. Growth can occur at temperatures as low as 0 °C, though as the temperature drops towards 0 °C the growth is slow. Listeriolysin damages human cells known as macrophages, which are involved in immunity. People with impaired immunity may have abnormally weak macrophages, which do not stand up to attack by the toxin of the listeria bacteria and permit the bacterium to move from the inside of the intestine to the internal organs.

One of the problems frequently encountered in tracing the source of illness caused by *Listeria monocytogenes* is that, unlike salmonella food poisoning, mass outbreaks of listeriosis are relatively rare. Among members of a wedding party who have eaten salmonella-contaminated mayonnaise, for example, perhaps two thirds will be ill within twenty-four hours. In such instances tracing the bacterium to the food is often successful. With listeriosis many of the cases are one-offs, and often occur among vulnerable patients, making tracking studies difficult. Furthermore, the incubation period – the interval between ingestion of the contaminated food and the appearance of symptoms – can be anything from five days to six weeks, by which time most contaminated food will have been thrown away. Soft cheeses can be kept for many weeks, so the linking of listeriosis to soft cheeses probably indicates the ease of tracing the infection rather than the overall importance of soft cheese as the source.

WHAT IS AN INFECTIVE DOSE OF LISTERIA?

There has been considerable speculation over what comprises an infective dose of *Listeria monocytogenes* – that is, how many bacteria are needed to cause disease and whether an 'acceptable level' in food can be identified. While it is true that certain foods containing about 1 million *Listeria monocytogenes* per gram have caused disease, we do not know if there is a safe level, for the following reasons.

- The risk from any food for any patient varies, and the vulnerability of the patient may be more important in deciding whether infection occurs than the numbers of bacteria eaten.
- The state of the bacterium, particularly the amount of its listeriolysin, may be as important as its numbers.
- When food is tested for *Listeria monocytogenes* the actual numbers of bacteria present may not be known because most of the methods used do not recover all the possible bacteria.
- The amount of contaminated food eaten can be unpredictable.
- Small numbers of *Listeria monocytogenes* initially in

food can multiply subsequently during storage in the factory, in the supermarket or in the home refrigerator before being eaten.

For these reasons the only logical approach is to aim for zero contamination of food; food that is ready for eating should contain no listeria at all. Because reheating of convenience food cannot be relied upon to kill all listeria, this sort of food should also contain no listeria bacteria.

FOODS THAT CONTAIN *LISTERIA MONOCYTOGENES*

It has been estimated that between about one tenth and one half of raw salads and chickens contain listeria. The numbers of bacteria are small, and certainly, as far as raw meat and poultry are concerned, conventional cooking and serving should eliminate them. As we have seen, the dangerous form of listeria occurs after it has grown at low temperatures. With this in mind, we can identify four possibly dangerous foods.

Salads

Prepared salads in which the vegetables are added to dressings or mayonnaise and then kept refrigerated for many days afterwards are a hazard. The dressings provide the nourishment needed for any listeria that might be present to multiply. Coleslaw is an obvious risk, but where the dressing contains high amounts of vinegar the food may be too acid for bacterial growth.

Soft cheeses

As cheese matures, there is a tendency for water to be lost, which results in the death of most bacteria. Hard cheeses such as cheddar would be expected to contain few, if any, listeria. It is difficult to be absolutely specific about the cheeses that could be dangerous. As a general rule, cottage cheese and processed soft cheeses have not been reported to contain listeria. The more risky cheeses are those made from goat's milk and ewe's milk, often sold in delicatessen shops. However, it must be stressed that many such cheeses are perfectly safe. Perhaps the greatest risk is from soft cheeses enclosed by a crusty skin such as brie or camembert. The problem for the buyer is to know which is safe, what tests have been done and whether contamination could have occurred after dispatch from the factory. Considerable research must be undertaken in this area.

The issue of whether the cheese has been made from unpasteurized or pasteurized milk is largely irrelevant because cheese made from pasteurized milk is capable of being contaminated during ripening, storage and transport.

The general hygiene of the whole cheese-processing operation would seem to be more important than anything else. At present about 10 per cent of soft cheeses contain listeria.

Salamis and other processed meats

These may be contaminated with listeria before or after manufacture, and long refrigerated storage may permit listeria to multiply to fairly high numbers. About 10 per cent of this type of product is contaminated with listeria.

Cook–chill

The typical cook–chill product in a supermarket is

either a cooked and chilled chicken, or a piece of one, or a recipe meal. The idea of this convenience food is appealing, in that meals are readily available for reheating at home or, in the case of chicken, eating immediately. The system involves the initial cooking of food to temperatures of about 70 °C, at which temperature all but the spores of bacteria should be destroyed. The food is then chilled rapidly and kept sufficiently cold to stop any food-poisoning bacteria from growing. The reheating is intended to make the food palatable rather than to ensure the destruction of food-poisoning bacteria – which should not be present anyway.

The problems begin with the transport and distribution of food in a chilled state, often through several staging posts. The temperature at which chilled food should be kept is ideally 0–3 °C, and the length of refrigeration may be anything from a day or two to three weeks. This complicated distribution and storage system is vulnerable to breakdowns anywhere along the line.

Other possible defects in the system include the failure of the initial cooking to destroy all dangerous bacteria, storage at too high a temperature on display shelves and incorrect treatment of the product after purchase.

However, cook–chill catering does have some advantages, notably that by separating the preparation of the food from the point of consumption it reduces labour costs. It provides the means to privatize institutional catering in local authority homes, schools and hospitals.

Unfortunately, commitment to cook–chill catering in supermarkets or institutions was generally made before the danger of food-borne listeriosis was appreciated.

Most institutions follow the Department of Health's guidelines of 1980, which were published a year before the first proof that listeria was food-borne. The food industry is a law unto itself, and its operating controls are much more lax than those proposed by the guidelines as far as both length of refrigeration and temperature control are concerned.

Several recent surveys have shown that cook–chill food is frequently contaminated with listeria. This is not surprising in view of the three essential features of this bacterium, which are its common presence in raw food and in the environment, its heat resistance and its ability to flourish, multiply and recover from heat injury under cold conditions. Our own data in Leeds have so far shown that out of nearly a hundred cook–chill foods from supermarkets nearly a quarter are contaminated with listeria. Others have found contamination ranging from 2 to over 50 per cent. A very large survey by the Public Health Laboratory service has shown that out of several hundred products from supermarkets 12–18 per cent contained listeria.

Recent figures from Leeds City Council are interesting. In its survey it showed that seven out of twelve cook–chill chickens that had been purchased from supermarkets some days after their first cooking contained listeria, whereas no listeria were detected in chicken pieces spit-roasted that day. The explanation for these different results is that it takes several days for the listerium bacterium to repair itself after being damaged by cooking.

Clearly, there is a problem with listeria in cook–chill products, and some suggestions for its solution will be given in Part II.

A TYPICAL CASE HISTORY OF LISTERIOSIS

Mrs E. R. was a 26-year-old mother of one girl aged 3. Her general health was good, and her first pregnancy and delivery had been normal. Mrs E. R. became pregnant again in 1988, and all went well initially. She continued to work full-time in the supplies department of the local hospital. When she was twenty-four weeks pregnant by dates and scan, she felt unwell after returning from work one day. She was sweating; she had a headache; and there was discomfort all down her back. She had no abdominal problems, and the baby was still felt to be moving.

When her husband returned from work – he was a manager in a store – he insisted on taking her temperature and found that it was 38.5 °C, more than 1 degree higher than normal. Because of the pregnancy, he phoned the surgery, and their doctor called in about two hours later.

The doctor confirmed that Mrs E. R. had a moderate fever and thought she was suffering from a urinary infection or had influenza. However, the month was July and none of Mrs E. R.'s contacts had had flu, so a sample of urine was sent to the laboratory. Three days later this was reported to be normal. During the next week the temperature and muscle pains persisted, both being worse in the early evening. The patient spent most of her time in bed and avoided any drugs for fear of their effect on the pregnancy.

Between the seventh and tenth day of the illness she felt slightly better, but on the morning of the eleventh day no movements were felt from the baby. At 8.00 p.m.

that day labour started. A dead baby was delivered at 4.00 a.m. the next morning. The blood from the mother and samples from the baby were tested for listeria in the laboratory. From each specimen *Listeria monocytogenes* was identified in two days. The appearance of the bacteria was very similar to that described in the introduction – small, shiny creamy-grey blobs were evident on the agar gels. Around the blobs or colonies the blood had decomposed as a result of the effects of the listeria toxin, listeriolysin.

What caused Mrs E. R. to acquire the listeria infection? During the six weeks before becoming ill, most of the food she had eaten had been traditional canteen food or, in the evening, home cooking; she had bought a ready-to-eat convenience meal from a reputable supermarket twice a week. These meals were not based on poultry and included no salamis or coleslaw-type products. However, she had eaten a number of English and imported soft cheeses. No remnants of the suspect foods could be found in the refrigerator or dustbin, and no other patients seemed to be affected at the same time. Thus while food was probably the cause of Mrs E. R.'s listeriosis and the loss of her baby, the item responsible will never be identified. Unfortunately, this usually tends to be the case.

6
Salmonella food poisoning

To most people food poisoning *is* salmonella – or at least it was until listeria came on the scene to pave the way for recognition of the many other types of food poisoning. Nevertheless, salmonella food poisoning has been the most comprehensively studied, and we can identify very accurately the huge variety – about 2,000 in all – of the different salmonella strains that can cause disease. Despite this, on many occasions it is difficult to pinpoint the infected food.

Salmonella bacteria are longer than they are wide and have on their surface hair-like structures that wriggle, so the bacteria can swim. The properties of these hairs and the bacterial surface vary in different types: *Salmonella enteritidis*, the commonest species now, is easily distinguishable from *Salmonella typhimurium*, the main scourge in the 1970s and early 1980s.

THE SOURCES OF THE DISEASE

The natural hosts of salmonella are generally birds and reptiles, although the bacteria may also be present in cattle, pigs and veal calves. Of course, salmonella can find its way into almost any food. In practical terms, it is poultry – chicken, turkeys and ducks – and their products that have caused us most problems.

Frequently salmonella lives in the animal or bird without doing any harm. In human beings, however, we should always view these bacteria as foreign and capable of causing disease.

Once people have recovered from salmonella food poisoning, they may continue to harbour the bacteria in their intestines and excrete it in their faeces. Such people are referred to as 'carriers'. If their personal hygiene is inadequte the salmonella may be transferred to other people, usually through food or, occasionally, in hospitals.

WHAT IS AN INFECTIVE DOSE OF SALMONELLA BACTERIA?

This question was studied experimentally in the USA by feeding volunteer prisoners different amounts of salmonella to see how many bacteria were required for them to become ill. (It is doubtful whether this type of experiment would now be considered ethical.) Results were surprising, in that between 1 million and 100 million bacteria were usually required to cause illness, and for healthy people that finding may generally hold good. However, much smaller numbers – thousands or even hundreds – have caused infection when present in certain foods, such as chocolate. Also small babies, the elderly, hospital patients and other vulnerable people may suffer food poisoning from quite small numbers of bacteria. Therefore, as with listeria, we must aim to ensure that the food we eat contains no salmonella at all.

One of the factors that decides how many salmonella bacteria are needed to cause food poisoning is the amount and strength of the acid in the stomach. The stronger the acid, the greater its ability to kill bacteria. Ill and vulnerable people, particularly babies, may have less stomach acid than is normal, so more salmonella survive the journey through the stomach.

THE EFFECTS OF THE DISEASE

A moderately severe illness begins between twelve and twenty-four hours after contaminated food has been eaten. The time lapse between eating the food and becoming ill is explained by the fact that the illness results from the growth of the bacteria in the intestine and the formation of a poison, known as an enterotoxin. The first feeling is nausea, followed by a colicky tummy ache, which comes and goes in spasms, usually all over the abdomen. This is followed by urgent and frequent diarrhoea, which is often watery and greenish, sometimes mixed with slime and blood. The patient usually feels hot or cold and sweats profusely. His mouth is dry, as he is losing fluid in the diarrhoea, but he does not feel inclined to drink. The illness is usually at its worst after six hours; after that the pains begin to lessen, and the diarrhoea becomes less frequent over the next few days. Exhaustion often lasts for longer than the diarrhoea, however, and full health will not return for some weeks. In most people the number of salmonella bacteria that are present in the faeces gradually declines over a few weeks, but in a few people the bacteria can persist for months or even years. Such people do not feel ill but remain a possible source of infection for others.

The above description is of a typical case of salmonella food poisoning. Some people may have a milder case and will not seek medical advice or take time off work. Others may suffer more severely. Those already described as vulnerable will be more likely to encounter complications than otherwise healthy people. In most people the salmonella remains in the gut, but occasionally it can get into the blood and cause a serious illness, referred to as blood poisoning or septicaemia. When this happens the temperature usually rises to 40 or 41 °C; the patient may collapse, be delirious and have difficulty with breathing. Some patients die from septicaemia – perhaps fifty to seventy per year in the UK. Even if antibiotics are successful in clearing the salmonella from the blood, the problems are by no means over, since it can get into the bones, the heart, the blood vessels, the kidney and almost anywhere else and can set up local infection that is difficult to treat. These complications account for a total of about a hundred deaths annually from salmonella food poisoning.

Salmonella food poisoning is a serious problem in the UK. About 250,000 cases of the disease are occurring each year. Many people feel ill for days or weeks, and the cost of working days lost, of treatment, and of tracing the sources is considerable.

THE SPREAD OF SALMONELLA FOOD POISONING

Sometimes salmonella contaminates food distributed to a large number of people: the consequences are alarming. In the UK our two biggest salmonella outbreaks occurred in 1984. One, at Stanley Royd Hospital, Wakefield, affected about 450 patients and staff. Nineteen vulnerable patients – long-stay elderly patients with psychiatric diseases – died. The cause – against the background of poor facilities, problems with the administration and staff morale – was a catering error: contaminated beef had been left out in the kitchen on a warm summer night. This case received a great deal of publicity. Less widely reported was the outbreak on British Airways aeroplanes the same year. There were 766 cases and two deaths. The source was apparently contaminated aspic glaze produced in a local kitchen as an accessory to a cook–chill system for the airline meals. The exact details have not been published.

Between 1983 and 1988 the number of reports by British laboratories of salmonella more than doubled; the increase has been wholly attributable to *Salmonella enteritidis*. By 1988, there were about 14,000 reports of the disease. (Remember that the real number of cases is probably ten times this figure.) During the first two months of 1989 the numbers of reports of *Salmonella enteritidis* were about double those for the correspon-ding months in 1988 despite all the public concern and the likely reduction in the numbers of eggs being eaten. There is no doubt that this is the worst salmonella epidemic experienced in this country – at least since we have been able to identify these bacteria – and it is still on the increase. This is certainly not a time for reassur-ance or complacency.

It has been suggested that the increase in figures for *Salmonella enteritidis* is due to greater efficiency in laboratories or in reporting, but the various procedures used have barely changed in ten years. In any case, this explanation could not account for the sudden increase in *Salmonella enteritidis* while the number of other salmonella-related cases has stayed about the same. Are patients more vulnerable now than they were? Possibly some people are a little more vulnerable, but others are healthier. Is the bacterium more dangerous, so fewer bacteria are needed to cause food poisoning? This would certainly be worrying, but the severity of the illness caused by *Salmonella enteritidis* seems very similar to that caused by other salmonella. Are we to blame for the contamination of the food we eat? There really is no reason to think that an acute deterioration in hygiene has occurred on a sufficient scale to account for these figures. And, if it had, why should it apply only to *Salmonella enteritidis*? An explanation could be that, by chance, a few large outbreaks have occurred recently and have distorted the figures. (The term 'outbreak' is a vague word to describe the simultaneous affliction of two or more people by infection from a single source.) Again, there is no evidence of this. Indeed, the number of outbreaks of salmonella food poisoning during 1988 was lower than in 1987.

During 1988–9 two major changes have been seen – a reduction in outbreaks yet an increase in the total number of reports of *Salmonella enteritidis*. Assuming that the size of outbreaks has remained more or less the same, the only explanation for these two apparently conflicting statistics is a substantial increase in non-outbreak incidents related to *Salmonella enteritidis*. In other words, we have to assume an increasing number of sporadic or one-off incidents. Since *Salmonella enteritidis* is almost entirely acquired from poultry meat or eggs, this evidence alone is highly suggestive that the rise in reports is due to contaminated eggs, which are often eaten as one-offs.

SALMONELLA AND EGGS

How salmonella gets into an egg

There are two ways in which salmonella gets into an egg: through the shell after the egg has been laid and during its formation in the chicken.

Shell contamination has been known for many years as a possible source of salmonella, which can pass from droppings to the inside of the egg through cracks or other damage to the shell. Indeed, washing the egg can cause the shell to lose some of its natural resistance to bacteria, so eggs are not normally washed before sale. It would be difficult to rid poultry flocks entirely of salmonella, but, obviously, the more salmonella present in the flock, the more the danger of shell contamination. There is no reason to think that this route for the spread of salmonella has increased recently, however. Even if the bacterium penetrates the shell, it has the barrier of the membranes on the inside of the shell to get through, and then it may not last long in the white of the egg because this contains a number of naturally occurring chemicals that damage bacteria. Most eggs – at least 90 per cent – are produced by the battery system. In this system the floors of the cages slope gently, so that the newly laid egg tends to roll to the bottom, avoiding contamination by droppings that pass through the wire mesh. So while shell contamination remains a source of salmonella in eggs, there is no reason to think it has increased recently, and certainly it cannot account for the phenomenal increase in *Salmonella enteritidis*.

It is the other form of contamination that must

provide the explanation. Salmonella is present within the egg-laying apparatus – the ovary and the oviduct – of the laying chicken and gets into the egg, both the white and the yolk, before the shell hardens. This method of bacterial transfer, referred to as 'transovarian', allows salmonella to be transferred from the female chicken to her offspring if the egg is fertile. The research showing the extent of this problem is impressive, although many egg producers refuse to acknowledge it.

What appears to have happened is as follows. Laying chickens have been carefully selected over the years by genetic experiment to produce what the customer wants – essentially, brown eggs that are available all the year round. Naturally, chickens lay for only part of the year, mainly in winter and spring, so the breeding stock – that is, chickens laying fertile eggs – has to be carefully 'designed'. Today breeding stocks are all fairly similar and are maintained by 'master' layers. It seems likely that salmonella is present in large quantities in the breeding stock, and if it is present in the egg-laying apparatus, it will find its way into some of the fertile eggs. (There is, of course, also the opportunity for shell contamination.)

The fertile eggs are transported to the hatchery, where the chicks emerge. The males are destroyed and the females sold and reared. If *Salmonella enteritidis* is present in a day-old chick, the chick may become ill with a general infection. Some chicks die in the first week or so of life. Many chicks recover. Unfortunately, the salmonella may not be eliminated; rather, it may find its way into the internal organs, such as the covering of the heart, the liver and the egg-laying apparatus, and it may persist there without doing any harm. The egg producer views his subsequent layers as healthy, even though the salmonella is lurking silently inside the chicken. The bacteria may not even be detectable in the droppings, so he may believe that the layers are 'free of salmonella' because the only way to demonstrate the presence or absence of contamination would be to kill the layer – obviously not economically a good idea!

This explanation for the recent spread of salmonella food poisoning is supported by experimental findings. Three large pieces of research have indicated the presence of *Salmonella enteritidis* in the internal organs of laying chickens, and the bacterium has been found inside eggs by several researchers who took care to avoid introducing the bacterium through the shell. This method of contamination does fit all observations and is the only plausible explanation for the inexorable rise in this disease in people. There is an urgent need to look at the breeding stock. It is not known at the time of writing (March 1989) whether the Ministry of Agriculture and the egg producers are determined to act in this area.

How many eggs are infected?

The month of November is a suitable month for statistics because holiday infections can largely be excluded. In November 1988 there were about 300 reports of *Salmonella enteritidis* every week, largely representing egg sources. We have seen that the real number of infections is probably ten times the number reported, so 3,000 people every week were getting infections from eggs. Since 30 million eggs were being eaten every day, we can calculate that if every infected egg caused food poisoning, then one egg in 70,000 was infected (30 million × 7 ÷ 3,000 = 70,000). But by no means everyone who eats an infected egg will get food poisoning: cooking may kill the bacteria; the numbers present may be too small; or disease may be thwarted by natural resistance. Possibly only one infected egg in ten causes illness in practice. If this is the case, the real incidence of salmonella-infected eggs is one in 7,000. This is not very high, you may think, and hardly worth all the fuss! But remember that the incidence of the disease has increased sixfold in the last five years, and we do eat a large number of eggs. My own responsibility is to prevent 2,000 patients in the Leeds hospitals from being infected. Since the calculations suggest that one egg in 7,000 is infected, and if each patient has an egg a day, two of the patients will eat an infected egg every week. Is this acceptable? No, it is not, and for this reason shell eggs were withdrawn from the hospitals in November 1988 and are still banned.

It must be stressed that among different flocks of laying hens the proportion of eggs that are contaminated will not be uniform, and there may be differences between types of egg production. At the moment there is insufficient information to claim that battery eggs are more or less likely to be contaminated than so-called free-range eggs.

Salmonella in chicken feeds

Until the egg debate gathered momentum most people were not aware that remnants of slaughtered chickens are recycled as feed for live birds. (It has been put to me that if the remains were not recycled, their disposal would present a problem.) This, regrettably, is not a new practice and is confined neither to poultry nor to this country. It is, however, instinctively repulsive and biologically dangerous.

The killing and preparation of the birds is done mechanically. This, incidentally, explains why so many raw poultry carcases (50–60 per cent) contain salmonella: it is because of inevitable cross-contamination. In general, the head, feathers and internal organs (the liver may be an exception) are recycled.

As a rule, the recycling of unwanted animal components occurs as follows. The remnants are transported to a processing plant, where they are converted to at least two usable products: fat, which is used in industry, and a protein-rich material that is added to the feed. Bacteria may well survive this process. The feed is often imported, and even if it is sterile on arrival in this country, it can be contaminated by vermin and wild birds. The consequence of these events is that the feed is frequently contaminated with salmonella and that any salmonella present in the internal organisms of the slaughtered birds may be ingested by live birds. It is no surprise that salmonella appears to have learnt to adapt to life inside chickens without doing any harm. Perhaps the only remarkable aspect of this is that it did not happen sooner.

Fortunately, there is now considerable concern about this practice, and some action over the contamination of poultry feed is being contemplated. I am sure that ultimately the feed must be made sterile, or very nearly so, by adding chemicals or through heat. However, for the *Salmonella enteritidis* problem at present such remedial steps will be too late, although cleaning up the feed will certainly produce nothing but benefit in the long term.

FOOD POISONING: THE BACKGROUND

The problem of tracing salmonella

Consider a person who eats for breakfast a fried egg that has been cooked so the yolk stays runny and then, during the following night, becomes ill with diarrhoea. Subsequently he is shown to be suffering from *Salmonella enteritidis*. How can the source of the bacteria be traced? There are numerous problems. First, the egg shells may have been emptied from the dustbin. Even if they are recovered, which egg shell corresponds to his egg? And if the infection has come from the yolk, there is unlikely to be any yolk adhering to the inside of the shell for testing.

Suppose we can show that a particular egg was the source of the food poisoning. Can we trace it to the farm and identify whether there is a major problem there? The answer is probably not, because the carton, if available, is likely to carry information only about the name of the packing station, the date of packing and the recommended sell-by date, the two usually being three or four weeks apart. So we should be able to trace the egg to the packing station, but will we be able to identify the farm? Rarely, it seems, as the packing station receives, sorts and grades eggs from a large number of farms. Our detective trail ends here. There is, of course, an urgent need for cartons to indicate exactly where and when the eggs were laid so that we can trace them back to source. The situation at present seems designed to protect the egg producer from this sort of scrutiny.

Because of the tracking problem, the source of many cases of food poisoning thought to be due to eggs cannot be proven, so the official figures released by the

72

Department of Health concerning the number of incidents of food poisoning caused by eggs are very much lower than the real numbers, even allowing for a multiplier of ten.

The answer to the egg problem

Unquestionably, *Salmonella enteritidis* is currently the largest salmonella problem we have experienced in this country. The problem is unique in two ways – both in the total number of people infected and in the rate of increase in the number of cases over recent years.

The simplest and most obvious answer is to identify and eliminate any infected breeding or laying birds. This, unfortunately, would be a difficult and expensive undertaking. However, if the problem goes on increasing in the future as it has in the past, then pressure will mount to enforce the measure. The infected birds will have to be identified by testing their internal organs, which could be done at the end of their active life. Once the infected flocks have been eliminated, they should be replaced by stock free of *Salmonella enteritidis*. There are already proposals for a constant testing programme that should prevent the problem recurring in the future.

However, the infected flocks have not yet been eliminated, the numbers of reports of *Salmonella enteritidis* are still increasing, and we should all still be wary of eggs. Advice about how to handle eggs safely will be given in Part II.

SALMONELLA IN OTHER FOODS

Almost any food that permits bacteria to grow can become contaminated with salmonella, which may be transferred from 'naturally' infected food – for example, in splashes from juices released by a thawing frozen chicken – or by human handling.

The thorough washing of hands after a visit to the toilet is essential. It is possible for bacteria to pass through most brands of toilet paper (toilet paper is designed mainly for its softness rather than as a barrier to bacteria!), and more than 1 million bacteria may be lodged invisibly around a fingernail. If food is prepared by someone whose hands are harbouring bacteria, salmonella may be transferred from fingers to food. The number of bacteria in handled food may be small, unless the food is kept in warm temperatures for some hours, when the numbers can increase rapidly. If that food is cooked thoroughly before eating, any contaminating salmonella will be killed. In practice, the most dangerous foods are already cooked poultry and meats that are kept outside a refrigerator for far too long or inside one with the temperature too high.

In summary, there is probably no moist food that has not been associated with salmonella food poisoning. Because of the huge increase in salmonella originating from eggs, we can anticipate a continuous problem with secondary causes. We must therefore attack salmonella on two fronts: we must eliminate it from raw food, and we must prevent secondary contamination by practising meticulous personal and kitchen hygiene.

7
Other food-poisoning agents

There is more bad news. Not only are there other serious causes of food poisoning, but over the last few years we have found some totally new ones.

CAMPYLOBACTER

This is the name for a group of bacteria that cause a particular type of food poisoning. Each can be identified accurately in the laboratory, but for practical purposes we can group them together here. They are fairly recently proven causes of food poisoning, having joined the official statistics only in 1980. Last year there were nearly 30,000 reported cases of campylobacter food poisoning, making it the commonest reported cause of all. This somewhat exaggerates its importance, since death from this kind of food poisoning is exceedingly rare.

The campylobacter bacterium is shaped like a tiny comma and occurs in contaminated poultry that is not adequately cooked, in unpasteurized milk and even in water. As with salmonella, campylobacter can get into other foods following contamination by raw food, particularly poultry. The disease is particularly common in warm summer weather, suggesting that bad hygiene is an important factor. Small children aged less than one year and adults in their twenties seem most vulnerable. Undercooked food eaten at parties on camping holidays or on visits overseas are mainly responsible.

The illness usually begins between three and ten days after suspect food has been eaten. It would seem that for disease to occur the bacteria must multiply so that they are present in large numbers in the intestine; it is not the eating of food containing pre-formed toxin that is the problem here. Recent medical research shows that some bacteria can survive well in acid conditions in the lining of the stomach, so it is possible that we can become ill after eating just a few of these bacteria, which survive the trip with the food through the stomach, and then multiply in the intestines beyond.

The course of the disease is rather different from that of other food poisonings, and it lasts longer because it is the presence of the growing bacteria that causes the disease rather than a toxin that may produce just a brief illness. The first effect is nausea, though there is no vomiting. Vague tummy aches and a fever of about 38·5 °C may last a day or so. Acute pains and diarrhoea follow and sometimes actual vomiting. Features of the diarrhoea are that it can be watery and contain fairly bright-red blood. Muscle pains and headache may occur, and sometimes the patient appears to be suffering from influenza. The illness lasts for five to ten days, and a further week or two will elapse before a return to normal health. During recuperation most people feel exhausted. Because the infecting dose may be small and the methods of identifying bacteria accurately are less certain than in the case of salmonella, tracking down the guilty food is not easy. Unpasteurized milk is still on sale 'at the doorstep' in some parts of the country, although it cannot be provided for schools and hospitals. In Lancashire and West Yorkshire perhaps 5 per cent of milk is drunk in an unpasteurized state. Those who prefer milk in this form are convinced of its better flavour and even better nutritional properties. Unfortunately, it is more likely to be contaminated with bacteria. Campylobacter is probably the commonest cause of infection from unpasteurized milk and should be entirely removed from milk that has been pasteurized. Those who defend the availability of unpasteurized milk point to the freedom of choice of the individual. However, campylobacter can sometimes be transferred from one person to another – for example, from mother to baby.

The control of campylobacter food poisoning is related to good hygiene, and the enforced pasteurization of milk before sale could be beneficial.

VIRUSES

Viruses are the smallest agents of infection known and consist of a core of nucleic acid, the hereditary material, a coat of proteins and sometimes other substances. Outside a human cell a virus is dormant, but once inside the cell it masterminds the cell processes for its own advantage and at our expense. The importance of viruses that may be eaten is that they can cause a disease very similar to food poisoning, although the food is blameless. In children a small, round virus causes vomiting, diarrhoea and abdominal pains. This disease, referred to as gastro-enteritis, can be mistaken for food poisoning; it can be caught from other children and, possibly, through the air. In adults the commonest problem with viruses is seen in hospitals or homes for the elderly. Over the course of a week or two, every day a few patients and members of staff will suffer from vomiting, tummy pains and sometimes diarrhoea. It is thought that such viruses are airborne, though they may also be spread by food that has been handled by someone with a virus. While it is impossible for these viruses to multiply in food, the disease they cause is similar to bacterial food poisoning, and they must be considered one of the possible causes of an outbreak of illness among a group of patients in a ward. The disease is usually mild and seems to clear up on its own.

Hepatitis, or infectious jaundice, is also caused by a virus and can be transmitted by contaminated food. A patient who suffers from this disease will generally become distinctly yellow; the colour is seen most obviously in the whites of his eyes. He may well feel sick, suffer from some diarrhoea and be off his food for weeks. It is rarely very dangerous, but the virus can be present in the faeces for some weeks. It can therefore get into food in two ways: raw or partly cooked fish, such as shell fish, may be contaminated by human sewage, and almost any food prepared by someone who is carrying the virus in his intestines may be contaminated. Thorough cooking should destroy the virus, so the riskiest foods are those eaten raw, such as prawns. In less developed countries disposal of sewage may not be as safe as it is in the UK, and some land-raised food may be contaminated by human sewage. Advice about sensible precautions can be found in Department of Health leaflets.

Other viruses, even those causing infantile paralysis or poliomyelitis, can all be caught from food, though rarely. There is not likely to be anything inherently amiss with the food itself, but the virus contaminates the food through contact with sewage or poor personal hygiene.

BACILLUS CEREUS – THE CHINESE RICE POISON

There are two types of food poisoning that are caused by *Bacillus cereus*, a bacterium found very widely in the environment, and often in food, that produces fairly tough spores that can survive boiling for a few minutes. The first type of disease resembles that caused by *Clostridium perfringens*. The illness starts about twelve hours after eating contaminated food and is characterized by diarrhoea and abdominal pains for a day or so. Probably more common is the food poisoning caused by cooked rice. Typically after two or three hours a feeling of nausea is followed by actual vomiting, which can be severe and may last for up to a day. Diarrhoea is uncommon, but patients feel exhausted for several days afterwards. This second type of illness seems to reflect modern eating habits, and fried rice from Chinese take-away restaurants is nearly always involved. It is certainly a recurring theme of this book that our desire to purchase food that is instantly ready to eat is risky.

Other types of rice are also possible dangers, though boiled rice may be kept hotter than rice prepared for frying just before serving. In the preparation of fried rice, the spores of *Bacillus cereus* that could contaminate the raw rice grains may well not be killed during the first boiling. Even if they are, the boiled rice may be contaminated after cooking. The boiled rice is usually prepared in advance, occasionally in large amounts, and allowed to cool slowly. This provides ideal temperatures for the dormant spores to change into growing forms of the bacteria. When the bacteria grow, they release their poisons, or enterotoxins, into the rice. The rice may be kept at room temperature for many hours, or it may be shifted backwards and forwards between the refrigerator and the warm kitchen whenever a portion is required. If this happens, the temperature may never be low enough to stop bacteria from growing. When a customer comes in to the reception area of a take-away and orders fried rice, a portion of boiled rice is transferred to the pan, some additions are made (such as raw egg and prawns) and the mixture is fried too lightly and rapidly to destroy most micro-organisms or their poisons. A pessimist would argue that this dish is a three-pronged danger: you could contract simultaneously *Bacillus cereus* food poisoning, salmonella poisoning from the egg and hepatitis from the prawns!

Methods of preventing this type of food poisoning have been suggested by Dr Richard Gilbert of the government food laboratory in Colindale.

- Rice should be boiled in smaller amounts and at frequent intervals during the day. It is obvious that all previous batches should be thrown away when a new batch is ready.
- After cooking, the boiled rice should either be kept at over 63 °C or be immediately refrigerated in small portions to ensure rapid cooling.

- Boiled or fried rice ready for sale should never be stored at temperatures between 15 °C and 50 °C and never for more than two hours at kitchen temperatures.

Certainly, if this advice were followed, the risks would be small. But can you see all take-aways using a range of thermometers and stop-watches? Sadly, much sound advice about food hygiene is ignored, and there are no laws to enforce any such recommendations.

VIBRIO PARAHAEMOLYTICUS POISONING

We are getting to the end of our catalogue of food-poisoning bacteria. The bacterium *Vibrio parahaemolyticus* is shaped like a small comma and has a long, whiplike tail that enables it to move rapidly in fluids. It can produce some poisons but is easily damaged by temperatures as low as 50 °C and will not grow readily in food that is on the acid side. *Vibrio parahaemolyticus* is naturally found in the sea, often in shallow water, mud and estuaries, and flourishes in the summer, so it may be present in raw fish, prawns, crabs, lobsters and oysters. In Japan fish is often eaten raw, and food poisoning from this *Vibrio* is quite common. In Britain it is rare. Simple hygiene measures, involving cooking fish adequately and ensuring that cross-contamination from raw fish does not occur afterwards, should be adequate.

The disease starts between twelve and twenty-four hours after eating contaminated food. Pain in the stomach comes and goes in severe spasms, and diarrhoea is urgent. Many patients feel sweaty and suffer from headaches. Although these symptoms improve over

two or three days, a feeling of tiredness can last
longer.

OTHER BACTERIA THAT CAUSE FOOD POISONING

For the sake of completeness mention should be made
of *Yersinia enterocolitica*, *E. coli*, cholera and *Shigella
sonnei*. These are either rare in the UK or are preventable by hygiene measures developed for other causes.

TOXINS FROM FUNGI AND CHEMICALS

These are mentioned only briefly, partly because there
is very little that the consumer can do about them, as
the problems arise before the food is purchased, and
partly because all are fortunately rare in the UK, at
least at the time of writing!

One fungus, *Aspergillus flavus*, produces a mould on
certain vegetables, nuts and fruits and has caused a
problem in some cereals fed to poultry. This fungus
can produce a chemical called an aflatoxin, which may
cause liver cancer. (A much more important cause of
liver cancer is Hepatitis B, a virus particularly common
in the Far East that is spread by sexual contact or by
injection.) At present, the real danger of aflatoxins is not
known, though there is agreement that food should not
contain large amounts of them, and batches of vulnerable food should be tested for their presence. Peanuts
and peanut butter have sometimes been found to contain high concentrations of aflatoxins. Careful controls
and monitoring are now in force, so these products
should be safe if bought from reputable suppliers.

Finally, a variety of toadstools, fish (puffer fish, some eels) and plants are naturally poisonous to us. Furthermore, unwanted chemicals can get into our food at various stages in its production.

The purpose of Part II is to show how we can ensure that our food is as safe as possible by minimizing the risk of bacterial poisoning. Risk has always to be considered along with price, convenience and nutrition; these will also be mentioned. It is hoped that those who are responsible for preparing food for themselves, for their families or for others will feel confident that the food is as safe as it can be. In Part I some examples of the dangers of poisoned food have been dramatic and may have caused some anxiety. Death from food poisoning is still rare, and we should not expect to suffer from food poisoning after every meal! Yet the last few months have seen real concern about our food safety. Food poisoning is preventable, although we may need to reconsider how we eat. Perhaps a little greater effort in buying, storing and cooking food will not only produce safe meals but also save money, and you may even enjoy your food more than you did before.

PART TWO

TAKING ACTION –
TODAY AND TOMORROW

8

In the supermarket

In this chapter we will make a trip around a supermarket and try to identify some possible problem foods
and how to shop safely. It may be worth while to take a
look backwards first to see how our shopping habits
have altered and how some of these changes have
caused our current predicament.

A typical home in the 1920s would not have had central
heating. The kitchen probably contained a solid-fuel fire
that provided room heat and a cooking facility. Food was
generally cooked slowly and thoroughly – and only once.
The kitchen contained no refrigerator or deep freeze: cool-
storage facilities were provided by larders, cellars or
pantries, and protection from vermin was afforded by
safes. Raw food was not stored for long, and cooked food
was soon discarded, so that the remains of the midday
Sunday joint were eaten that evening in sandwiches.
After that the domestic pets were given the scraps!
Because of the difficulties of storing food, shopping was
done many times a week, often daily, and most people
bought their food at local grocers, butchers, greengrocers
and fishmongers. In many ways food and eating were
treated with more respect than they are today. No one
planned for instant meals whose production and consumption were subservient to the television. The meal time was
the central gathering point of the family.

In the last fifty years our patterns of shopping, cooking and eating have become totally different. Convenience dominates our lives now. Many people shop just once a week at a single food shop – the all-embracing supermarket. Most new supermarkets are being built now as part of leisure or general shopping complexes that demand an enormous amount of space, notably for car parking. New developments therefore generally occupy out-of-town sites. It may require a lengthy trip to buy our food, and it is not surprising that we are loath to make this trip frequently, particularly if there is a long delay at the check-out. Of course, the price of many standard items is less than that of goods purchased from small local shops, and it is the cheapness of the food in the supermarkets that has been one of the attractions for so many customers. The appeal of shopping infrequently is particularly relevant to working women. However, infrequent shopping means that many items have to be stored for days or even weeks, either deep-frozen or in refrigerators.

Our cooking habits have also changed out of all recognition. Speed, not thoroughness, is all that seems to matter, be it with microwave ovens, or with fan-assisted ovens, or with other devices (for example, those designed to produce toasted sandwiches). The availability of microwave ovens has been a major factor in encouraging the choice of convenience meals.

Despite these enormous changes in the way we eat – and we have not yet mentioned the fashion for eating out – controls and legislation concerning food safety have hardly altered over the last thirty years in the UK. Some of the current risks from food poisoning reflect our requirements for cheap, instant meals, and we must

How Foods Decompose

Food	Causes of deterioration	Effects
Vegetables	Loss of water in storage, actions of enzymes in the vegetable, attack by bacteria and fungi	Limpness, dullness of colour, brown edges, wet rot, slime, spots of brown/ grey/yellow colours, bad smells, especially cabbages
Fruit	Loss of water in storage, attack by fungi and sometimes bacteria	Soft rot, brown/ grey/ green/pink areas, wrinkles, wet areas, bad smells
Fats, particularly in margarine, creams, some cheeses	Oxygen and spontaneous breakdown of fatty acids	Products go 'rancid', unpleasant smell, taste not too impaired. Polyunsaturated fats more vulnerable than saturates
Meat	Decomposition by own enzymes and surface bacteria	Colour changes from fresh pink or red to grey-green. Production of ammonia, leading to putrefaction and food poisoning
Fish	Surface bacteria, particularly due to *Pseudomonads*	Occurs more rapidly than with meat and at lower temperatures, with fishy ammonia smell and decomposition of flesh

look critically at intensive rearing, food-production processes, the supermarket, our storage at home and our cooking methods. An inspection of a modern branch of a highly respected chain of supermarkets will reveal both good and bad aspects of our available food.

FRUIT AND VEGETABLES

We first enter the fruit and vegetable area. It is this department that gives us most optimism for the future and has seen enormous improvements over the last few years. The range of products that are always available is impressive: we can buy loose or packaged items, and an increasing array of exotic fruits and vegetables is displayed. There is also some organically grown produce. Excellent. But it is not possible to state that organically grown produce is necessarily safer than traditional vegetables; each item should be looked at individually.

Vegetables and fruit may decompose from the action of their own enzymes, which degrade the structure as a continuation of ripening, or they may be attacked by bacteria and fungi. Fungi are a particular problem for acidic fruits. Fungal and bacterial rots often begin on the outside of the fruit or vegetable and can appear as discoloured areas. *Penicillium* mould is a blue-green colour; *Botrytis* is a grey mould; *Aspergillus* is usually black. Colours from cream, to brown, to nearly pink can occur.

The best way of testing the quality of the fruit and vegetables is by simple inspection. Look at each intended purchase carefully for any imperfections. This is much more important than buying within 'sell-by' dates or checking whether the product has been displayed on refrigerated shelves. After all, we have no idea of the history of the product before it got into the shop. For example, how did those Chilean raspberries get to the UK looking so fresh? Inspect items for coloured blemishes (including around the stalks), for loss of texture, limpness suggesting long storage, general colour and any cuts into the fruit or vegetable. Age is usually indicated by brown, ragged edges.

In our supermarket the appearance of all the whole items that had not been cut was uniformly favourable – we did not find a single product in an unsatisfactory condition. However, some of the prepared items, such as the cartons of cauliflower florets, looked a little tired and some of the mixtures of salads in cartons enclosed in Cellophane appeared to be on the point of decomposition, with some grey-brown discolouration and general limpness. These would probably be satisfactory for immediate eating, but after a few days in the home numbers of bacteria could be quite high, and the poor flavour and texture of the product would have to be disguised by dressings. One of the practical problems with these prepared salads is that they are difficult to wash, whereas if they are assembled in the home, the vegetables can be easily washed before preparation.

THE FISH COUNTER

At the end of the vegetable area the fish counter boasts a wide variety of raw fish, some fairly exotic. The fish are in containers on ice, so at least their undersides are cold. The temperatures on the upper surfaces may be moderately high – say, 10 °C – because there is no enclosure around the fish, and heat will come from the lighting and the air. Most people believe that fish taste best if cooked immediately after being caught. This may not actually be the case and is in any event usually impossible to achieve in reality. Perhaps fish taste best after they have been kept for between one and three days at a temperature of 5–10 °C. The most obvious indication of fish that have been kept for too long is their smell; as decomposition occurs, so ammonia and other nitrogen-containing gases are given off. The fish become alkaline, limp, fragile and dull. Changes in the eyes occur so rapidly on storage that most fish bought will have whitish eyes.

Fortunately, many of the bacteria that grow on stored fish are fairly harmless to us. These are mainly *Pseudomonads*, which grow at temperatures of between 5 and 10 °C. Cooking the fish will kill the bacteria, but they may have already caused decomposition of the fish, with its associated fishy smell, and loss of firmness and flavour may be experienced after cooking.

On approaching the fish counter, the smell is positive but not unpleasant, and there is little ammonia. All the fish are looking in good shape. They are shiny and appear just right. But what is that in the middle of the counter? Two large, unwrapped, whole smoked salmons, looking very appealing, are separated from the other fish by two small plastic ridges about 5 centimetres high. We do, of course, usually eat smoked salmon without cooking and we know that, as a matter of principle, food ready for eating should not be kept adjacent to raw food. The danger here comes from the bacterium *Vibrio parahaemolyticus*. This may well be present on the raw fish, and it is quite possible that, during their handling, bacteria could drop on to the smoked salmon. In the raw fish the *Vibrio* should be killed by cooking, as it is very sensitive to heat. But what happens to the *Vibrio* in the smoked salmon? This depends on how the salmon is kept. If it is kept at room temperature overnight or in a refrigerator that is not cold enough, the numbers of bacteria could increase to dangerous levels. *Vibrio parahaemolyticus* can grow at temperatures as low as 8 °C, and the temperature in many domestic refrigerators will be above this.

This is an unfortunate blot on an otherwise excellent department. The simple solution is to make sure that the storage, manipulation and sale of ready-to-eat foods such as smoked salmon is physically separate from raw food and that different staff are employed for each type of product. If this is too costly, then pre-packed smoked salmon is essential.

Buying and storing fish

What to look for
* Raw fish well chilled, preferably on ice.
* Fresh smell, no trace of ammonia.
* Shiny skin, firm appearance.
* Separation of raw items from products ready for eating, in both location and handling; smoked salmon must never be stored with raw fish.
* Cleanliness of server, particularly fingernails; hand washing.
* Ask where and when it was caught.
* If filleting is done, it must be done in its own dedicated area.

Storage
* At home fish should be unwrapped, stored on a

deep plate or receptacle in a refrigerator away from cooked food.
- Fresh fish should be eaten on the day of purchase.
- Fresh fish should not be frozen.
- If frozen fish is purchased, it should be transferred to the deep freeze within one and a half hours of purchase. If it has thawed, it should be cooked and eaten immediately, not refrozen.

CANNED GOODS

Among the canned produce, many varieties of food are useful for emergency meals – for example, a can of the supermarket's own brand of macaroni cheese, which provides two servings. The can is not dented, there is no evidence of rust and it is not bulging, so it should be as microbiologically safe as anything can be. The label lists details of ingredients, calories and main nutritional classes. These are carbohydrate, fats and proteins. Interestingly, the label also gives microwave heating instructions. Is canned food the answer to our demand for instant meals that are safe? And does it enable those of us who bought a microwave over a year or two ago to find a use for it now? One important point about this product is its price, just 41 pence. Of course, canned food may be deficient in some vitamins such as vitamin C, so we should not eat this type of product exclusively. There are many other excellent canned foods available in most supermarkets, such as canned tomatoes and baked beans. (You may, however, be surprised at the sugar and salt content of some varieties.)

CRISPS

In the next section of our supermarket is the most impressive display of crisps we have ever seen. From the bacteriological viewpoint, these should be safe and can be kept at ordinary room temperatures. Their safety is related to their low water content, which makes them hostile hosts for bacteria. If the bags are penetrated and damp air enters, the crisps will be soft and, in an extreme case, slimy. Very slight softness should not pose a danger. We look at two large bags, each notably an assortment of six standard-size bags. In the first the ingredients are described as 'organic potatoes, sunflower oil, natural flavouring and sea salt'. In the detailed analysis of the nutritional values every 100 grams is stated to contain 36.0 grams total fat, of which 24.0 grams are polyunsaturates. The sunflower oil will have provided almost all the polyunsaturates, and there is good medical evidence that polyunsaturates protect people against heart disease and strokes. Unfortunately, one of the problems with food high in polyunsaturated fats is that, on storage, these fats tend to decompose more rapidly than saturated fats. Associated with this decomposition can be poor flavours and a smell that becomes almost rancid over weeks. Polyunsaturated fats can be converted chemically to typical animal saturated fats by adding hydrogen: these are described on the label as hydrogenated vegetable oils. This process does two things: it converts the fat from a vegetable type to an animal one, and it improves the keeping qualities of the food. This is one example of problems generated by the infrequent purchase of items that require prolonged storage and, therefore, the addition of food preservatives.

Let us look at another bag of crisps – the company's own brand. The label tells us that the ingredients are 'potatoes, vegetable oil including hydrogenated vegetable oil, salt'. The typical total fat component in each 100 grams of the product is 38 grams, of which just 12·0 grams are polyunsaturates. The amount of polyunsaturates is therefore half that of the other brand because a considerable proportion of the vegetable oil has been hydrogenated – in effect, it has become animal fat.

Tips on buying and storing crisps, biscuits and snacks

- Ensure that bags and cartons are not damaged.
- The proportion of polyunsaturates in the total fat content is the important statistic to look for – the higher, the better.
- 'Hydrogenated vegetable oil' means, effectively, animal fat.
- Do not be impressed by claims that any product is 'natural'. Crisps and biscuits and their ingredients are artificial, man-made products and are not natural!
- Crisps, biscuits and snacks should not be soft when purchased.
- Store in airtight containers in the home.
- Long storage may lead to rancidity.

COOKING OILS, BUTTER AND MARGARINE

We must be extremely careful about products that contain vague descriptions of 'vegetable oil' or 'hydro-

genated vegetable oil'. There is even one naturally occurring vegetable oil that is extremely high in saturated fat
and low in polyunsaturates. This is coconut oil, also
referred to as palm oil. It is rarely available in the
pure state in the UK, although it can be used in making
peanut butter.

From the medical point of view, there is no proof that
the differences in the fats in corn oil, groundnut oil,
rapeseed oil or even olive oil, if you can afford it, will
affect health. However, when buying cooking oils, you
should avoid products whose labels do not indicate the
exact source of the oil or the fraction that is polyunsaturated, since it could be high in palm oil. On this trip to
the supermarket we noticed one oil product made from
'blended vegetable oils'. Because of its high content of
polyunsaturates, pure corn oil would be preferable.

Many of these points apply also to butter and margarine, so look at labels carefully.

'Low-fat' products are being promoted at present. In
general the reduction in fat in margarine, for example,
results from the presence of water, carefully added so
you cannot see it. These 'low-fat' products seem, on the
whole rather expensive.

Points to watch out for

- Always check labels for the exact source of oil and
  the proportion of its content that is polyunsaturated.
- Avoid products that contain coconut (palm) oil,
  which is high in animal-type saturated fats.
- The phrase 'low fat' on food labels should not be
  taken at face value. The key fact to ascertain is the
  amount of polyunsaturates.

EGGS

On arrival at the egg station in our supermarket it was gratifying to see that, quite correctly, the eggs were not stored in a chilled cabinet.

We looked at a carton of free-range eggs. There were details of the packing and sell-by dates on the top and a picture of two chickens in an open field. There was also the statement: 'Store in a cool place. If stored in a refrigerator, remove thirty minutes before use.' We wondered how many people do this. (This problem will be discussed in more detail in Chapter 11.) On the carton was the statement: 'These eggs are laid by hens which are allowed to roam and feed freely, obtaining a proportion of their food from natural sources.' This does not, of course, mean that all free-range eggs are laid by hens scratching about in fields and farmyards. In the standard free-range system the chickens spend most of their life packed close together on the floor of a shed but are sometimes allowed to escape into a small pen, although it is not certain whether many in practice do so. We do not know on what type of farm these eggs were laid.

Before buying eggs, open the carton and inspect each egg for cracks, damage, soiling by droppings or other visible defects in the shell. The absence of these does not guarantee that there is no salmonella inside, of course, but it does lessen the risks of bacterial contamination in general. If the shell is damaged, bacteria other than salmonella can get into the inside of the egg and create the real bad egg. Not only is the smell of a bad egg unbelievable, but the white and yolk are often inseparable and may be a repulsive colour – anything from green and pink to brown or even black.

Buying eggs – points to note

- Ignore any claims that flocks of laying hens are salmonella-free.
- Free-range eggs are not necessarily safer or better to eat than battery-produced eggs.
- Many free-range units contain laying chickens that are tightly packed on shed floors, with tiny pens outside.
- Eggs should be stored at room temperature in the shop.
- Look for the packing and sell-by dates.
- Examine each egg for soiling by droppings, cracks or blemishes.
- Eggs should not have been washed.
- Imported eggs are not necessarily safer than those from UK sources.

RAW MEAT

Among the poultry on display there was a good selection of raw chicken, some whole and some in portions, ducks and turkeys. Beef, pork and lamb were also available in various joints and forms.

Every item was wrapped. This is not necessarily a desirable procedure. While it can enable the buyer to examine the product thoroughly, the wrapping may influence the growth of bacteria immediately under it. Moreover, if the wrapping is impermeable to gases produced during decomposition of the meat, the give-away smell of a product that is 'off' may be missed until the wrapping is removed.

The meat was stored on chilled shelves. There were only a few temperature gauges. The temperature control of whole meat items is not quite as strict as that of processed products because any bacteria should be confined to the surface and destroyed rapidly in cooking. Some of the products, however, had clearly been made from reassembled meat. These are typically labelled 'turkey roasts', 'pork roasts', etc., are usually of a regular cylindrical shape and may contain water and gels in the middle. It is quite difficult to cook the inside thoroughly without drying out the outside, as the fibres of the various meat muscles are arranged in random fashion. These products always pose a greater food-poisoning threat than non-processed meat because bacteria that might become dangerous are transferred from the outside of the meat to the inside during their assembly.

Minced meats, which were also available, are not recommended because of the uncertainty of their exact composition.

Buying meat – points to note

* Avoid processed or reassembled joints (often of uniform shapes).
* Check on sell-by dates, and cook and eat accordingly. The ideal time for eating red meat is after it has been hung for some days.
* Poultry joints are sometimes 'improved' by seasoning (described by the trade as added value – for them!). Ask yourself whether this is really worth the extra money.

- Avoid minced beef, pork, lamb – you do not really know what is in it. So-called '100 per cent beef' could include the lungs, liver or even brain (see Chapter 15). I suggest you prepare your own mince – it should be safer, and you'll know what's in it!

CHEESE

The next area we looked at was the cheese department. The shelves were refrigerated. As in the case of raw meat, the temperature controls do not have to be as rigid as for other products. Indeed, we do not really know the ideal storage temperature for soft cheese if we wish to discourage the growth of listeria. It can be argued that at a temperature of 3 °C listeria alone will be able to grow. At higher temperatures – say, 10–12 °C – other, harmless bacteria may grow and interfere with listeria; on the other hand, bacteria capable of causing food poisoning may grow. We cannot win! At the moment we have to view soft cheeses with suspicion, mainly because of the risk of listeriosis. Simplifying the problem, we can generalize thus.

- The harder the cheese, the lower the risk of listeria.
- Vulnerable people, notably pregnant women, should not eat soft cheeses. Some processed items may be relatively risk-free, though this is not to recommend these.
- The more complex the product, the greater the risk of contamination.

BACON AND SAUSAGES

Along from the cheese department is the bacon section. The pig has got off lightly recently! Few food-poisoning incidents have been linked to pig products, one reason being that preservatives are commonly used. A pack of the supermarket's own brand of smoked bacon contained 'Pork, water, salt. Preservatives: sodium nitrate, sodium nitrite. Antioxidant: sodium L-ascorbate'. The principal preservative in this list is sodium nitrite, which prevents the growth of certain spores, such as those of *Clostridium botulinum*. There is no evidence that small amounts of these substances are harmful. This particular pack had a 'best before' date of six weeks from that day – surely an unnecessarily long interval?

If you require bacon to last for six weeks, it must be preserved and sealed in the pack. If you do not want to eat preservatives, you should buy preservative-free bacon from the butcher, if you can get it, and treat it with the same respect as you would other raw meat. The two types of product look the same, and their taste is similar, but they must be treated in totally different ways.

Next to the sausages, still a favourite of the British. (Why?) We preferred the supermarket's own brand of thin pork sausages because penetration of heat into the centre is more certain than in the case of large bangers. The label proudly boasts 'No added colours' and 'No artificial flavouring'. As a consequence, the colour of the sausages is a pale buff. The label states that they contain a minimum of 65 per cent pork, yet only 15 per cent of the product is protein. This suggests that some of the ingredients from the pig must be low in protein. The label admits to 'Preservative: sodium sulphite'. The sausage is another example of products that require preservatives if we want to store them for any length of time. The 'best before' date is in four days' time; although we are not notified of the date of production, it could have been several days ago. Surely the consumer has a right to know exactly when this and other products have been assembled or prepared?

RECIPE MEALS

There are a variety of attractive packets containing recipe dishes, or parts of dishes, to be eaten after reheating. The packets contain such items as Chicken Korma, Cauliflower Cheese, Beef Stroganoff and Chicken Tikka and are stored on lit shelves. In the case of some chicken products the dish can be eaten without reheating. These are the products that are giving many people anxiety at present.

The wrapped whole chickens look attractive and give the appearance of having undergone a very recent, thorough roasting. Most of these products have not been roasted in the conventional way but steamed, then covered with burnt sugars to give the impression of roasting. The trouble with the production of cooked chicken is that ordinary roasting followed by storage for, say, seven to ten days causes drying out and shrinking, though this problem can to some extent be resolved by adding to the meat polyphosphates that cause uptake of water. The temperature gauge on the shelves shows 6 °C, but the actual temperature on the surface of the chicken could well be higher, perhaps 10–12 °C.

We pass on to more cook–chill products, described as 'fresh' soups. These are presented in most attractive packaging, but the price – £1·20 or so for two portions of soup – seems high. Also is 'fresh' the right word?

These products may have been prepared a week ago and have since probably undergone initial cooking, chilling, storage, transport and distribution before reaching the supermarket's shelves.

Points to consider before buying a chilled or recipe meal

- The temperature controls on open shelves are not strict enough.
- The product may be a week old before you see it.
- The meal may be infected with food-poisoning bacteria. If it is stored in a domestic refrigerator whose temperature is inadequately controlled, the bacteria will multiply and the danger presented by the food will increase.
- Microwave reheating may not destroy listeria.
- Poultry is riskiest. The term 'roast' may denote steaming rather than true roasting. The brown colour of chilled 'roasted' chickens is conferred by burnt sugars (glucose, dextrose, sucrose or caramel), which should be listed among the ingredients on the label.
- About a quarter of chilled whole chickens and chicken-based recipe meals may contain listeria.
- The price of these products is high.
- Why not buy safer and cheaper alternatives?

FROZEN FOOD

We pass on to the deep-frozen foods. Here, as in supermarkets elsewhere, there is a great deal of promotional activity designed to persuade the customer that 'freshness' is obtained through the storage of foods under refrigerated conditions. Always treat the label 'fresh' with suspicion.

The frozen food here is stored in open and lit cabinets, the temperature of which should be between $-18\,°C$ and $-23\,°C$. Few temperature gauges are visible, as all are about half way down the cabinets, and products are piled high above the tops of the cabinet. (Presumably this is the result of rummaging by customers.) Frozen peas and broad beans seem good, safe buys; these and other items should be selected from the bottom of the deep freeze because the temperature is lower here than near the top.

Frozen foods should be transferred to a domestic deep freeze within one hour.

DRIED FOOD

Dried food should be safe as long as the packets are intact and are kept carefully after opening. The best-value rice appears to be the brown American long-grain rice, although it requires fifteen minutes of boiling. Surely this is worth the effort? We can also recommend some Italian pasta, *tagliatelle verdi*. While there has been a report of pasta contaminated with *Staphylococcus aureus*, this must be rare, and the bacterium does not cause fatalities.

BREAD AND CAKES

The bakery department, like the fruit and vegetables section, has been very much improved in recent years. Bread has moved away from the formerly uniform array of loaves made from bleached flour to a varied selection of all sorts of bread and rolls, some baked on the premises. In our supermarket it was difficult to see any risky products in the bread area, although in the middle

there were some moist potato scones that contained preservatives!

The same was true of baked cakes and pastries. If
there is danger associated with these, it is their fillings.
Jam that is high in sugar should be safe, but insist that
all cream is really fresh – in the true sense of that word.

THE DELICATESSEN COUNTER

We needed to check the last department carefully –
the delicatessen counter. The staff seemed to be maintaining a high standard of hygiene. Generally, however,
the purchaser has no idea when foods such as pâtés
were made and whether their storage temperatures are
correct.

In summary, this supermarket was in the top league. It
exuded confidence (but not music); it was busy; the
quality and variety of many items were excellent. Apart
from soft cheeses and eggs, which both present problems that are still to be solved, the only products
capable of causing safety problems were those that
were never intended to be purchased during occasional
visits to the supermarket – the bacon, the cook–chill
recipe meals, the cooked chicken, the 'fresh' soups. If
customers demand the availability of these products,
they must accept either the use of preservatives or the
risk of microbial contamination.

9

Storing food in the home

Once your food has been bought, there are three possible ways of storing it at home – at room temperature, in a refrigerator or in a deep freeze. The labels of some products may carry the instruction 'Keep cool'. This does not help very much today. 'Cool' storage is a vague term, signifying a temperature somewhere between refrigeration and room temperature, say, 10–15 °C. This is ideal for certain products such as cheeses and would have been the temperature in old-fashioned pantries or cellars.

STORAGE OF CANNED, DRIED AND PRESERVED FOOD AT ROOM TEMPERATURE

Canned food can be stored at any temperatures between 0 °C and 30 °C, but do not put a can in the deep freeze – ice formation could burst the container. Most cans do not have an expiry or 'best before' date because for any individual product this will vary according to the temperature. Cans last for the shortest times under warm, moist conditions, which can cause rusting. But most should be safe for at least six months. Under average conditions many cans could last some years, and although this may result in some change of flavour, the product should be safe as long as the three golden rules of cans are observed: no bad denting, no rust holes, no bulging. Dried food such as wheat flour, cornflour, rice, lentils and breadcrumbs should keep well as long as they are dry. This means that, ideally, the packets should be stored in lidded biscuit tins. At the very least the packets should be kept in dry cupboards, away from the floor, so attack by pets, vermin, insects and beetles is unlikely. Attack by insects and beetles is not common in the UK, although it is in tropical countries. (I can recall vividly the repulsion of opening a packet of chocolate bought in the Philippines which, on unwrapping, was found to be full of holes and small, black creatures.) If dried food becomes wet as a result of damage to the packet, bacteria can start multiplying. If, for example, flour becomes moist and does not run freely, it should be discarded.

Cans or jars of pickles, sauces, ketchup, mayonnaise and other dressings may or may not contain enough substances such as vinegar to prevent bacterial growth. Before opening these can be stored at room temperature; after opening it is safest to store them in a refrigerator unless the wrappings advise otherwise. Generally, however, they should be treated according to the five-day rule and discarded after that.

THE REFRIGERATOR

Most refrigerators are cooled by chloro-fluoro-carbons (CFCs), which are thought to be causing damage to atmospheric ozone. The release of this coolant in the home is exceedingly unlikely; CFCs get into the atmosphere during the manufacture and disposal of the refrigerator. When you consider buying, or replacing, a refrigerator check on the coolant and avoid CFCs.

Refrigerator temperatures

The ideal refrigerator temperature is that which prevents the growth of all food-poisoning bacteria. Because of the resistance of listeria, this temperature must be as low as possible – between 0 °C and 3 °C (though even at this temperature listeria may not stop growing completely). Butter, margarine and cheeses may not be satisfactory at this temperature if eaten immediately on withdrawal from the refrigerator; they will be hard and will lose some of their taste and smell. (Two refrigerators, one kept at 0 °C and one at 10 °C, would be the answer, but that is not a practical proposition for most of us.) Dairy products should perhaps be removed from the refrigerator an hour before use to allow their flavour and softness to return. This is a safe practice but not always easy to remember, particularly early in the morning.

Checking the temperature of a refrigerator

A temperature of 0–3 °C must be our objective for safety, and we must be able to tell what the temperature actually is. Few refrigerators have built-in temperature gauges (why not?), so a thermometer is needed that reads in the range − 5 to + 10 °C. This should be placed near the middle of the fridge – it could be taped to one side – so that the temperature can be read easily on opening the door. Some refrigerators may not be able to reach these low temperatures; if yours cannot, perhaps you should consider buying a new one. The temperature should be checked after the door has been closed for some time, such as first thing in the morning.

Defrosting and cleaning a refrigerator

Most refrigerators need little maintenance other than regular defrosting according to instructions. A good time to do this is on the day before shopping day. Clean the inside with an ordinary detergent and water. The important aspect of cleaning is to remove all visible food remnants, splashes and stains. Bleach or other antiseptics should not normally be used. It is important to check regularly that the door seals are intact and that the door shuts easily and tightly. Leaving a refrigerator door ajar overnight could be dangerous.

Storing refrigerated food safely

The organization of the food in your refrigerator is important. The cardinal rule is to separate raw and cooked food completely. Ideally a refrigerator should have a partition that ensures this separation. If yours does not, you will have to use different shelves for raw and cooked food. The danger that arises from contact between raw and cooked food is that bacteria present on the raw food will contaminate cooked food; drops of blood from meat joints, for example, must never be allowed to fall on to cooked food. A simple expedient is to store raw food at the bottom of the refrigerator and cooked food at the top. Each of the stored items should be individually wrapped, and they should not be jammed too close together. In an overcrowded refrigerator there may be a long interval before the temperature drops to ideal values after loading. Moreover, some items may be tucked away out of sight, and consequently forgotten, which could lead to dangerously long storage.

How long should food be kept in a refrigerator?

The question of how long items can be stored safely is a difficult one. It depends on the quality of the temperature control of the refrigerator and the nature of the food itself. Let us assume that we do our major weekly shopping on a Saturday. The following Friday we should defrost and clean the refrigerator in preparation for the next week's food. It follows that most of the stored food should either be eaten or discarded on Thursday, so no more than five days elapse between stocking and disposal. Even if the refrigerator has an automatic defrost cycle, the five-day cleaning rule is a good practice. (I wonder whether the automatic defrost facility might be leading us into bad habits.)

This general rule needs to be modified for a number of items, of course: unopened wrapped cheeses, bacon and other packeted products may be safe for longer than five days. However, it is vital to adhere to dates on packaging and to ensure that the temperature of the refrigerator is always as low as it should be.

Other products should not be kept in a refrigerator even for five days. Milk and cream (which should be pasteurized), opened cans, left-overs, cooked meat, some salads, fresh mayonnaise and sauces should generally be stored for up to two days only. Some products, such as custard and gravy made from powder, should not be kept at all.

Should eggs be stored in a refrigerator?

There is now complete confusion over whether eggs should be stored in a refrigerator. Advice from the Department of Health in 1988 that we should do so seems extraordinary for the following reasons.

Recommended Maximum
Refrigerator Storage Times

Food type	Storage time
Raw food	
Whole joints (not processed), to be cooked thoroughly	3–5 days
Sausages, mince, offal	1–3 days
Bacon (no preservative)	3–5 days
Bacon (with preservative)	According to packet instructions
Vegetables and salads	1–5 days, according to appearance
Fish	12 hours
Cooked food	
Meat, poultry, ham, pies, stews	2 days
Vegetables	Avoid
Gravies, sauces, custards	Never
Opened cans	2 days
Dairy products	
Milk and cream (pasteurized), unopened	2–3 days
Milk and cream (pasteurized), opened	2 days
Cheeses	According to packet instructions or for as long as the appearance is acceptable

The purpose of refrigeration is to stop dangerous bacteria from multiplying. Once bacteria are present in food in large numbers, cooling them down will not reduce those numbers. If refrigeration is to be successful, it has to be applied immediately to vulnerable food. It would, for example, be highly dangerous to refrigerate, and subsequently to eat, the left-overs of a beef joint that had been kept at room temperature for two weeks. But this is exactly what is being proposed in the case of eggs. The contamination of eggs occurs, as we have seen, either before laying or soon afterwards as a result of droppings that stick to the shell. The eggs are transported from farm to packing station to shop, where they are kept at room temperature. Perhaps ten or fifteen days will elapse before the egg is bought. If the inside of the egg is contaminated, bacteria will have multiplied to achieve their maximum numbers well before the purchase of the egg. But can refrigeration of eggs do any harm? The answer is yes, on two accounts.

First, the egg shell, while appearing to be a solid structure, has many tiny holes that are plugged naturally. If eggs are washed, these plugs can be removed and bacteria can penetrate the shell. Because the inside of a refrigerator is usually moist and condensation can occur, water may drip on to eggs stored inside it. This can have the same effect as washing, in that the plugs can be dissolved. That is why egg producers and packers do not wash eggs.

The second problem involves cooking. If an egg is boiled, fried or poached after being stored in a fridge, the temperature of the yolk will be lower than it would have been if it had been stored at room temperature. This means that it is harder to kill salmonella present

113

in an egg yolk after refrigeration than after storage at room temperature. (Further thoughts on the safe cooking of eggs are offered in Chapter 11.)

Eggs should be stored at room temperature for, ideally, no longer than a week after their sell-by date.

Correct refrigerator management

- Install a thermometer in the middle of the refrigerator.
- The temperature should be between 0 °C and 3 °C.
- Check the temperature just after the first daily opening of the door.
- Clean the inside at least once weekly to remove all remnants of food or spills.
- Check that door seals are intact weekly.
- Separate raw and cooked food completely, with cooked food at the top, raw at the bottom.
- Wrap items individually, and leave space between them.
- Opened cans (or their contents), cooked meats, milk, salads, fresh mayonnaise and sauces should be kept for two days only.
- Do not store eggs in the refrigerator.

THE DEEP FREEZE

The ideal deep freeze is a cabinet type and is not combined with a refrigerator. True, in small kitchens there may be no alternative to an upright combination unit. However, the low temperatures required by the deep freeze are best maintained by a cabinet-type freezer because when the lid is opened the cold air does not 'fall out', as it does with an upright type. A thermometer

is advisable, and the required range of temperatures is
-18 °C to -23 °C.

Deep freezing arrests all growth of bacteria, but it
does not kill them, and risks can occur if food is
contaminated before re-freezing after slight thawing.
Items of deep-frozen food generally have a star rating:
one star suggests that the product is satisfactory for
just one week; two stars indicate that one month is
safe; and, more usually, three stars suggest that a safe
period is three months. The times refer to an acceptable
quality of flavour, taste and texture rather than the
possible growth of bacteria, so these storage times are
guides and can be extended if the quality is acceptable
to the individual (which distinguishes the freezer from
the refrigerator, in which storage should not exceed the
recommended periods on account of both quality and
the risk of bacterial growth).

Defrosting your freezer

A deep freeze will occasionally require to be defrosted
unless the model possesses a built-in defrost cycle. The
intervals for defrosting will vary according to model
and use. A simple policy could be adopted: every three
months the freezer should be cleared of all food, defrosted, cleaned and then restocked with three-star products. Home produce is often frozen, however, and the
anticipation of three-monthly food requirements is
fraught with difficulty.

Labelling and rotation

The way that food is rotated depends on the organization of baskets and shelves inside the freezer. What
should be avoided is the addition of new packets at the

top, followed by their immediate use. Label every item and indicate when it was placed in the freezer. Purchased deep-frozen items should also carry the date on which they were stored.

Every item should be wrapped to prevent cross contamination. For example, home-made ice cream (not, of course, made with raw egg) must never come into contact with raw poultry, meat or fish. One section of the deep freeze should be dedicated to the storage of sweets and other items not requiring further cooking.

Thawing frozen foods

First take out of the freezer the item in question. The product should be in a polythene bag. Remove it from the bag and place it in a container that confines any juices that emerge on thawing. In the case of poultry, don't try to extract the giblets yet. Put the food in the bottom half of the refrigerator, so that if any juices are spilt, they will not contaminate other food, and so that if thawing is complete some hours before cooking, the cold temperature should prevent bacteria from growing. A cool room at a temperature of, say, 15 °C can be used if available. Microwave ovens can be used according to instructions, but a refrigerator is preferable. (The problem with microwave defrosting is that, in effect, the food is cooked lightly from the outside in. The surface dries out, and the penetration of heat to the inside is uncertain.) The giblets of poultry should be removed when possible, and cooking should begin when there is no evidence of ice crystals in the inside of the bird.

Guide to Thawing Poultry

Method	Size of poultry	Appropriate thawing times
Refrigerator	Small chickens, pieces	1 day
	Large chickens, ducks, small turkeys	2 days
	Large turkeys	3 days
Cool room	Small chickens, pieces	12 hours
	Large chickens, ducks, small turkeys	1 day
	Large turkeys	2 days
Microwave	Small chickens, pieces	8–15 minutes* (standing time 10 minutes)
	Large chickens, ducks, small turkeys	15–30 minutes* (standing time 20 minutes)

* Approximate. Please read instructions.

Living safely with a freezer

- Cabinet types are preferred.
- A thermometer should be installed and should read ranges between −18 °C and −23 °C.
- Packets should be identified and marked with date of purchase and/or freezing.

- Stock rotation within the star-rating scheme should be planned.
- Items with only one month's life should be at the top of a cabinet-type freezer.
- If items are stored for longer than recommended, loss of quality of the product will ensue rather than danger.
- Frozen sweets or other items ready for eating must be stored apart from raw meat, fish, poultry and vegetables.
- In the event of a power cut, do not open the lid of your freezer. On restoration of power, any thawed items should be discarded.

10

Hygiene – personal and in the kitchen

If you read nothing else, read this.

This is a guide for everyone involved in food preparation in the home. Even stricter advice applies to caterers, restaurateurs and food factories. These are the minimum safety procedures.

PERSONAL HYGIENE

What you should do	*Why you should do it*
Wash your hands frequently	To remove bacteria that might cause food poisoning or spoilage of food
– on entering the kitchen	To remove bacteria picked up elsewhere
– after using the toilet	To remove bacteria that can pass through toilet paper on to fingers or from moist groin areas
– after handling any raw meat, fish, poultry, vegetables or possibly contaminated food	Because these items can harbour bacteria
– after cleaning kitchen surfaces, sinks	To get rid of any bacteria
– after disposal of food into waste bins	Contact of the hands with waste bins can pick up bacteria

Use bar soap that is kept dry between uses	This prevents bacterial growth on wet soap
Use a nylon nail brush, and keep it dry between uses	Bacteria around fingernails and in crevices are difficult to remove, so brushing is needed
Replace nail brush monthly	Nail brushes can pick up debris over the weeks and provide breeding ground for bacteria
Dry hands with a towel that is used only for this purpose – never use a tea-cloth	This prevents bacteria from being transferred from hands back to utensils
Change hand towels daily	This prevents the build-up of bacteria and moisture that may contaminate hands after drying
Ideally, use one kitchen sink or basin for hand washing and another for food preparation and dispersal	To prevent cross-contamination
Cover cuts and lacerations on arms, hands and face with waterproof plaster	To prevent your blood from getting into the food
Keep hair under control, for example with slides or ribbons	To avoid contamination of food with floppy locks

Avoid touching your hair, nose or mouth	This could transfer your bacteria to the food
Bathe or shower and change clothes regularly	To reduce the number of bacteria that are dispersed from the body and clothes
Remove rings and watches	To permit thorough washing of hands, wrists and forearms
Do not prepare food if suffering from food poisoning or diarrhoea	To avoid the risk of transferring food-poisoning bacteria to the food. With severe diarrhoea it is difficult to maintain perfect hygiene
Keep nails as short as you can	This reduces the risk of bacteria lodging in fingernails
Clothing should not be too loose	To avoid possible contact with food
Wear an apron made of wipeable material for messy jobs such as filleting fish	If any contamination does occur, the apron can be wiped clean and hung up to dry

KITCHEN HYGIENE

What you should do	*Why you should do it*
Always keep raw food – meat, fish, poultry, vegetables – separate from cooked food	To prevent bacteria from raw food being transferred to cooked food

If raw food does accidentally touch cooked food, consider reheating the cooked food or discarding the 'soiled' part	To remove any bacteria that may have contaminated the cooked food
Use separate areas for preparing raw and cooked foods	This reduces the risk of contamination of cooked food by raw food
Ideally, use separate knives and other utensils for raw and cooked food. If separate utensils are not available, wash and dry the utensils thoroughly each time raw food has been manipulated	This reduces the risk of contamination of cooked food by raw food
Try to prepare already cooked items before raw food	This reduces risk of contamination of cooked food by raw food
Have two chopping boards, one for raw foods and the other for cooked meats, and label them	To ensure that raw and cooked foods are always separate
Change hand towel, tea cloth and dishcloth daily	Bacteria can multiply on most fabric
Keep pet food in a separate section in the kitchen or in the refrigerator, and use different utensils to prepare it	It is good general practice to keep pets and their food separate from human food

Always clean slicers, graters and processors thoroughly after use, then dry

Remnants of food can support the growth of food-poisoning bacteria

As a kitchen cleaner, use hot water and a detergent for brushing and wiping

The answer to kitchen hygiene is not to splash antiseptic everywhere but physically to remove food debris and dirt from surfaces and crevices

Repair any deep crevices around the sink. Chopping boards that are deeply scored should be discarded

Food remains in deep crevices can harbour dangerous bacteria

Protect food all the time from pets' interest

Pets may contaminate food with their bacteria or transfer bacteria between raw and cooked food

Make sure the kitchen denies access to flies, other insects and beetles

These can all transfer bacteria between foods

Keep all rubbish bins firmly lidded

Pets, vermin and flies may transfer bacteria from them to food

Immediately remove any excreta from pets

To prevent possible contamination of food

Check regularly for damage to packets of dried food or spills from containers or fluids

Spillage of food encourages vermin and moisture may permit bacterial growth

Food kept in the open should be covered	To prevent flies and other pests from alighting and transferring bacteria between items
Never leave cooked food outside the refrigerator for longer than one and a half hours	This period, the so-called 'lag phase' of the bacterium, is usually 'permitted' because the numbers of bacteria will not increase much in that time
Ideally, the kitchen temperature should be the lowest that is comfortable. Ventilation may be required to keep the temperature down	The lower the temperature, the less the risk of multiplication of bacteria
Empty the waste bin before it overflows. Seal each complete load and place in dustbin	If waste falls out of an overloaded bin, this could be teeming with bacteria and dangerous
Maintain the fabric of the kitchen. Pay attention to the floor, walls, storage cupboards and doors	To deter pests and to remove hidden food remains

11

Safe cooking and eating at home

GENERAL TIPS ON SAFE COOKING IN THE HOME

- Buy fresh, whole produce of high quality.
- Buy food thermometers. Aim to keep temperatures below 10 °C (cold food) and above 63 °C (hot food). Between those temperatures lies the range within which many food-poisoning bacteria grow, although listeria will survive at temperatures below even 10 °C. Incidentally, remember to wash thermometers well after use – it would be most unfortunate if a thermometer were to cause food poisoning.
- Estimate the cooking time of each item on the menu in advance. Plan how the oven space and each ring or burner is to be used. (The idea behind this approach is to minimize the time during which food must be kept warm after cooking.)
- When tasting food during cooking, use a clean spoon, then wash it thoroughly. *Never, never* use fingers for tasting!

The purpose of cooking is to alter and improve the texture, taste and smell of food *and* to render it microbiologically safe. It does not entail the total elimination of all bacteria, but it does ensure the removal of those that are harmful. The growing forms of spore-forming bacteria should be destroyed, as should bacteria such as salmonella, listeria, *Staphylococcus*, *Vibrio* and viruses such as hepatitis. Cooking should also decompose any toxins in food. Heating food to a temperature of 70–80 °C is likely to achieve most of these objectives if the heat is applied for long enough. Lower temperatures may produce the same results if the food is cooked over longer periods.

The conditions needed to kill bacteria are similar to those required to damage the cells that make up the food, be they animal or vegetable. This breaking down of the cells is marked by a change of colour – for example, from red to brown in meat, or from dark green to light green in cabbages – by a change of texture (the food becomes softer) and by a change of smell and taste. To rid food of possibly dangerous bacteria we could apply a rigid formula – cooking for so many minutes at a certain temperature for a certain size of food. Alternatively, instinct and experience tell us when an item is cooked.

COOKING ON A HOB

Boiling and frying

Assuming that adequate penetration of heat occurs, the most certain way to destroy food-poisoning bacteria is to boil or fry food. In general, the penetration of heat into food is much more rapid in hot fluids than hot air. The temperature of boiling water is 100 °C and that of hot fat about 140–180 °C. In conventional ovens heat penetrates food more slowly. For example, if you boil a saucepan of sprouts for fifteen minutes, the inside temperature of each sprout will eventually be 100 °C; a dish of cauliflower cheese baked in the oven for forty minutes with an air temperature of 200 °C may have a central, or core, temperature of no more than 50 °C, although the outside may be golden-brown. Boiling vegetables until they are soft but not disintegrating should kill any dangerous bacteria.

Shallow- or deep-frying small or flat items until the outside is crisp and the inside looks and tastes cooked should also be safe. From the nutritional point of view, it is best to use sunflower oil for frying. Change the oil frequently, and remove any excess oil with kitchen paper before serving. Frying larger items, such as the fashionable 'jumbo' sausage or large pieces of chicken, requires care. If heat is to penetrate adequately into the centre, the surface may be overcooked. The problem is compounded by the use of coatings (breadcrumbs and other ingredients), which may burn easily. To get round these difficulties, fairly slow cooking is required, and the item should be turned several times if fried in a shallow pan.

Eggs: dos and don'ts

How do you cook eggs safely? In the Microbiology Department at Leeds University some experiments with different types of egg cooking have been performed, and the temperatures reached after cooking have been found to vary enormously. All the eggs had been stored at room temperature before cooking. The highest temperatures reached were in omelettes cooked in hot fat at 160 °C and in large pans, and the lowest temperatures were recorded in the centre of the yolks of normally boiled and fried eggs. Scrambled eggs cooked until firm and well-cooked omelettes and soufflés should be relatively safe. Ordinary cooking of boiled, fried and poached eggs and of lightly cooked scrambled eggs

Temperatures of Egg Yolks
After Cooking

Cooking method	Central temperature
Placed in boiling water for 3–4 minutes until white solid, yolk runny	45–50 °C
Frying in fat at about 150 °C until white solid; occasional basting	35–45 °C
Poached eggs placed in boiling water until white firm	50–60 °C
Scrambled eggs (runny)	65–70 °C
Scrambled eggs (firm)	75–85 °C
Omelettes cooked until solid	75–90 °C
Cheese soufflés baked in oven until centre firm	80–90 °C

would not be expected to eliminate salmonella, however.

As salmonella bacteria are generally found in the yolk of an egg rather than the white, a general rule for cooking eggs is that the yolk should be cooked until it is pale yellow and hard. This may take seven or eight minutes for a boiled egg, and it is extremely difficult to achieve it with a poached egg. Fried eggs turned and cooked on both sides may be safer than when cooked on one side. But even these precautions do not ensure complete safety, as well-cooked eggs have been associated with salmonella food poisoning. The advice for the elderly (those over 65), people who are ill, pregnant women and babies under one year is that they should avoid eggs altogether except in baking. It is most regrettable to have to proffer this advice, since these are the very people who might find lightly cooked eggs of benefit to them. Clearly, those who are vulnerable should also avoid foods made with raw or very lightly cooked eggs (see p. 135).

Gravies, custards, soups and stocks, sauces

These are often made partly or entirely from powdered ingredients, which may well contain large numbers of bacteria. They will not present any danger as long as they are not allowed to grow. When making up these products, try to get the temperature up as high as possible, although it may be difficult to raise the temperature of custard above 80 °C. The hot fluids should be stirred thoroughly and used as soon as possible – certainly within an hour and a half of mixing. It is essential that any left-overs are discarded because of the risk that contaminating bacteria may begin to grow. If powdered ingredients are added to stocks, it is advisable to discard left-over stock as well.

Safety points

- Boiling and frying are the most certain methods of destroying bacteria, viruses and toxins in food.
- Large items should be fried slowly and turned. Coatings may make thorough heat penetration difficult.
- Cook eggs until the yolk is pale yellow and firm.

Well-cooked scrambled eggs, omelettes and soufflés
should be relatively safe.

- Cook mixtures made from powdered ingredients at
as high a temperature as possible, and stir thoroughly. Discard left-overs.
- Wash pans and utensils carefully.

COOKING WITH A CONVENTIONAL OVEN

In the oven the penetration of heat will depend on the
size of the item. In the case of big joints of meat or large
poultry the outside must be protected by foil, fat (often
streaky bacon) or metal containers in order to prevent
burning before heat penetration occurs. Poultry present
a particular problem because the inside of a carcase
may be contaminated with salmonella or campylobacter.
In order to kill the bacteria the free circulation of air is
essential. Stuffing should never be placed inside poultry
for roasting but should be cooked separately in a flat
dish. When roasting large joints a sensible procedure is
to leave the cover or wrapping in place for, say, two
hours and then to remove it for the last thirty minutes
so that the meat can become brown and crisp. It is also
reasonable to use a low heat (e.g. 150 °C) for a fairly
lengthy time (say, three hours), during which the meat
is covered, followed by a short burst of cooking at,
say, 250 °C, when the meat is uncovered. (No attempt
is made to give exact times or temperatures because of
the enormous variety of ovens.)

A meat thermometer may be used to take the inside
temperature of a cooked joint. It should be 70–80 °C or
higher. Alternatively, a traditional method is to insert a

skewer; if the juices run clear, adequate heat penetration should have occurred. This method is not as scientific as a temperature reading, but it is based on the knowledge that when blood is heated to temperatures needed to kill bacteria it solidifies, so cannot run back out of the small holes made by the skewer, whereas fat that has been liquefied by the heat can do so.

Safety points

- Brief baking, even in a hot conventional oven, may not remove bacteria from the inside of large food items.
- Poultry should be roasted slowly, and protection of the outside by foil, fat or baking tins may be necessary.
- Stuffing should not be inserted into the cavity of poultry.
- A meat thermometer should show an internal temperature of at least 70–80 °C at the end of cooking.

MICROWAVE OVENS

Microwave ovens have a use in the home, though it is limited. The ovens are part of the convenience revolution and, in general, should not be relied upon to destroy bacteria in food: experiments have shown that both salmonella and listeria in food can survive microwave reheating. Microwave ovens act through the agitation of molecules in the food, particularly those of water. The waves themselves do not have any effect on bacteria; it is only the heat generated by the agitation of molecules that may destroy the bacteria. This occurs only on the surface of the food, however – perhaps to a depth of

2 centimetres or so. The penetration of a large item by the heat occurs slowly, by means of conduction – that is, heat is gradually diffused through the food – and it is most unlikely to kill bacteria in the centre. Moreover, the waves produced may not be uniform, so cold spots can occur, even just under the surface of the food, particularly in older models. (A rotating platform overcomes this problem to a certain extent.)

Heat penetration to the centre of items can be improved if they are left in the microwave oven for some minutes after active heating. During this time, however, there is a loss of quality of taste and smell. I have noticed with microwave cooking that some items tend to become hard (for example, sausages and bacon) and other items soft (for example, the burger bun in Chapter 12).

Microwave ovens should not be regarded as the simple solution to all food preparation; rather they should be used principally to heat or reheat food that is known to be bacteriologically safe. They cope most satisfactorily with potatoes for baking, the heating of gravies and sauces made from powders or granules and the reheating of *recently cooked* meals for latecomers.

Safety points

- Microwaves themselves do not kill bacteria; only the heat generated by molecular agitation is capable of destroying bacteria or toxins.
- Only the surface of the food is actually heated. The rest of the food is warmed by conduction. The process is slow and should not be relied upon to rid food of bacteria.

- Microwave ovens are ideal for heating sauces, drinks and soups made from 'safe' ingredients and for re-heating recently cooked food that is safe.

CHILLED AND FROZEN CONVENIENCE MEALS

These products cannot actually be recommended because of their indifferent quality, high cost and, in the case of chilled meals, possible microbial contamination. Nevertheless, many people are determined to eat them – and the packets are pretty.

Chilled convenience meals should be avoided altogether by vulnerable people – the elderly, pregnant women and people with general illness, particularly if their immune system is affected. Such meals may contain listeria, and the poultry-based meals are most risky. For the rest of you, all I can recommend is that you adhere to the manufacturer's instructions, whether you are using a conventional or a microwave oven. When the meal has been cooked for the prescribed length of time, take the temperature of the food at the centre. If it is less than 80 °C, cook the dish for a few minutes longer. The snag here is that the quality of the product may deteriorate. One of the continuing uncertainties about chilled meals is that we do not know what conditions are necessary to eliminate any listeria that may be present.

RAW FOODS

Fruit, salads and some vegetables are eaten raw. We can take a few straightforward steps to ensure that all are safe.

First, buy these products unprepared or unprocessed (see Chapter 8), so that you can see the whole item, undisguised by dressings. Remove unwanted stalks, roots or leaves with a sharp knife. Then remove any areas of rot, discolouration or softness. Wash each item thoroughly in cold running water (if necessary, wash each lettuce leaf individually). Dry with a clean tea cloth.

The suggestion has been made that salads should be washed in diluted bleach to remove any listeria. This should not be necessary.

If you have combined vegetables in a salad, it is wise to keep the dressing or mayonnaise separate, in its own container, and to allow each diner to apply the dressing as required. This permits the optimum storage of the dressing, either unopened in a cupboard or, if opened, in the refrigerator. It also enables a salad to be assembled some time before a meal (though probably not more than twenty-four hours). If salads are made in advance, they should be kept in the refrigerator.

Shellfish such as prawns, which may be contaminated by human sewage, pose a problem. In some countries they are irradiated as a safety precaution, but this process is not legal in the UK. If shellfish are to be eaten raw, very thorough washing is essential after the removal of the shells. But, ideally, they should be cooked.

Finally, a word about eggs. The dangers inherent in eating raw eggs are now generally accepted: *no one should eat a raw egg*. Very lightly cooked eggs are no less risky – foods containing these should also be avoided. The following list, which is not comprehensive,

includes some everyday items to which you should give
a wide berth.

Drink

egg flip (eggnog)

Meat

steak tartare

Sauces

béarnaise
hollandaise
mayonnaise
mornay

Sweets

baked alaska
egg-custard sauce
egg-jelly sponge
floating islands
fruit chantilly
ice cream (home-made)
lemon meringue pie
mousses (also savoury)
orange snow cream
queen of puddings
vanilla honeycomb mould
zabaglione

If these have been purchased from commercial
sources, pasteurized egg may have been used in their
preparation, though you will not know this for certain.
In any case, there is some doubt whether the pasteurization of eggs is always effective in eliminating salmonella.

Safety points

- Buy fresh produce of high quality.
- Remove any discoloured areas, stalks and unwanted
  parts with a clean, sharp knife.
- Wash thoroughly in cold running water.
- Apply dressings or mayonnaise to salads on in-
  dividual plates.

- Place opened mayonnaise or dressings in the refrigerator immediately after use.
- Regard raw shellfish with suspicion. Wash them thoroughly.

12
Eating out

FAST FOOD

The nutritional content of some fast food leaves quite a lot to be desired, and it is not my intention here to recommend this type of food. Assuming you are planning to eat this food, however, it is important that it should be safe: that is, it should not be likely to cause food poisoning.

Burgers

Let's start by looking at how a typical cheeseburger is prepared. The muffin or bun has been recently baked (we hope), is low in water and is unlikely to support the growth of food-poisoning bacteria. The round of minced beef, with its additives, must have been prepared in advance but has probably not been cooked. Ideally, it has been stored, deep-frozen, in its own wrapping, which is peeled away. The beef is then cooked on a very hot, greased plate. It should be cooked on both sides, and the colour of the meat should be brown throughout. As it is flat, there should be good penetration of heat, and this cooked product should be safe.

The cheese presents no special microbiological problem because it is processed, and garnishes of pickles or tomato sauce should not be risky if opened containers have been stored correctly, under refrigerated conditions. Be wary of sauce containers that are obviously old, with dried crusts around their caps. They may have been out for days or even weeks.

In theory, the cheeseburger should be a safe food, as should other burger types.

Fried chicken

While small pieces of chicken are probably generally well cooked, which means that salmonella will have been destroyed by heat, large pieces of chicken (e.g. legs) could pose problems if they are cooked for instant eating from deep-frozen storage. A number of options are open to the caterer. One is to thaw out items in advance; this is not entirely satisfactory because of the uncertain numbers of the orders to be anticipated. Alternatively, items can be thawed rapidly in a microwave oven, then deep-fried. Here there is a risk that the inside will not be properly thawed by the end of the cooking. Or chicken legs can be cooked in advance and stored, chilled, ready for reheating; again there is a risk that the inside will not be cooked adequately. Another possibility is that chicken legs could be prepared for cooking, then kept chilled (not frozen) pending demand. The raw food may be contaminated, and the handling could add further bacteria. If such products are kept for some days, listeria bacteria could multiply. Their destruction will always depend on the final cooking.

One of the problems for consumers is that they do not know the history of the components of the fast-food meal. Try asking: you'll probably get a frosty reception! Confidence in a fast-food outlet rests very much on its cleanliness, planning and hygiene and on the grooming of the staff.

The doner kebab

The kebab is made from minced meat, with various additions, which is moulded by hand – literally – around a vertical spit that rotates in front of a heat source. As the outside is cooked, slices are shaved off; these are usually eaten in bread. This instantly available food is risky. The raw minced meat will contain numerous bacteria – as many as 1 million in every gram would not be surprising. The added ingredients may aggravate the contamination as could the handling by human hands. Furthermore, during cooking some uncooked part of the kebab could be sliced away.

The greatest danger, however, is that bacteria such as *Clostridium botulinum* may grow in the centre of the kebab, which may never get really hot. If the kebab is little used on one day, reheating on the next or subsequent days could result in the sale of dangerously contaminated food, and the addition of unused warm kebab to the next day's product would be even riskier. Neither of these events should occur, but commercial pressures may overrule good catering principles.

Take-aways

At least with the kebab you can see it before buying a slice. In the case of most take-aways, particularly Chinese or Indian, the food production is invisible to the customer.

Menus can be astonishingly comprehensive. While this is due, to some extent, to the addition of different sauces to similar items, which extends the choice, the instant availability of such a range of dishes suggests that many are kept hot for long periods or chilled and reheated in microwave ovens. These procedures are not inherently dangerous, and if batches of food are prepared at frequent intervals (say, every two hours or so), the risks are small. Similarly, if food is kept chilled for a day or so under controlled conditions, it may be safe. The opening hours of a take-away are a useful guide. Those that open for one or two limited periods each day are probably safer than those that open all day, which may resist the temptation to discard food kept for a long time. The cleanliness of the premises and the grooming of the staff are important indicators of concern about food safety.

Fish-and-chip shops

These are safe! To my knowledge, no bacterial food poisoning has ever been traced to fish-and-chip shops. In general, everything is done correctly from the point of view of food safety. The fish is fresh or, possibly, deep frozen; it is cooked thoroughly once in hot fat; it is usually cooked to order; and it is served and eaten immediately. There is no processing, storage or reheating of the fish, and chips are rarely associated with food poisoning.

The pub

Public houses are gradually escaping from their image of the exclusive resort of the beer drinker. Not only have the hours become more relaxed, but also children are being tolerated in at least some areas, and the provision of food is the number-one profitable activity. Pub food (sandwiches or 'ploughman's lunches') is as safe as its components. The danger items are mayonnaise and dressings. Large opened jars should always be stored in the refrigerator; pickled items should be safe at room temperatures. The pork pie and the Cornish or meat pasty need special attention, however.

A pork pie is made from an open pastry case into which a minced-pork filling is inserted. A pastry lid is then applied. The lid has a hole that permits, after baking, the entry of a gel to fill the space created by the shrinking of the minced pork during cooking. The risks of a pork pie are posed by the gel, which is a perfect growth medium for bacteria, and by the minced pork. The temperature of the gel, when introduced into a pie, is not very hot, and it can introduce bacteria to the inside of the pie. Proper storage is of paramount importance in preventing these bacteria from increasing in large numbers. Ideally, a pork pie should be stored under refrigerated conditions, though some people dislike eating cold pies. If a pie is stored at room temperature, the risks increase with time. Pity the person who suffers from vomiting and diarrhoea the day after an evening session in the pub and gets criticized for excessive drinking, when the real cause was the *Staphylococcus aureus* and *Clostridium perfringens* in the pie! (Incidentally, gastrointestinal illness from alcohol-containing beverages is likely to be the result of drinking too much alcohol, pure and simple, although it is easy to blame wrong 'mixes'!)

The Cornish or meat pasty may be more dangerous than the pork pie because it will probably be stored warm. This is one area where legislation is urgently needed. Some pubs fill their warm cabinets with pasties for the lunchtime sales at about 11.30 a.m. This practice may not be dangerous if the food is eaten by 1.00 p.m. But when should the warm pie be discarded as potentially dangerous? In practice, it may not be until the end of the day, and we all know that the sight of available food makes us want to eat it. (There is a well-studied nervous pathway through the eye to the brain and then to the stomach.) So what should the customer do? In the relaxed atmosphere of the pub he or she could ask for the history of the pasty. Otherwise assume the worst, and do not eat a warm pasty after 1.00 p.m.

The motorway service station

There are two types of food, typical of restaurants in motorway service stations, that may cause problems. One is the vat of soup; the other is the warm meals (e.g. all-day breakfasts), kept warm under strong lights. In both of these cases the temperature (usually 63 °C) may not be high enough to stop food-poisoning bacteria from growing. It is difficult to know when the foods were cooked and first placed under the lights. With solid foods drying and shrinking may suggest prolonged reheating, but with soup there may be little to go on. As in many other catering establishments, the customer has to rely on the local staff.

EATING OUT AT A RESTAURANT

Before looking at a specific menu, some general comments may be helpful. First, the preparation of food in front of customers is a general indication that the restaurateur has nothing to hide. Second, the more cooks you see, the more likely it is that each of the courses is being prepared from fresh food. Third, the cleanliness of the staff and the general hygiene of the restaurant suggests concern with food safety. In the absence of much specific legislation concerning food storage, a dirty restaurant may have to be prosecuted by the local environmental health department on the grounds of defects in its structure — walls, floors, etc. — because these are visible, although the real risks concern food handling and hygiene matters. The customer too has to assume that the invisible hygiene of food preparation and storage corresponds with the general ambience of the restaurant. In one of my favourite restaurants in Leeds everything is right. The kitchen is staffed by many people; the pizzas are made on the spot, in front of your gaze; the hygiene is excellent; the ovens heat to very high temperatures; each pizza is assembled to individual order, and it is served immediately after cooking, usually within ten minutes of ordering.

Let us now look at a typical menu of restaurants in the middle–high range of quality. The month is March. The starters could include the following items:

Avocado vinaigrette
Avocado with prawns
Duck-liver pâté and brown toast
Soup of the day
Egg mayonnaise
Pancakes à la maison (containing sea food, asparagus
and herbs in a cream sauce)
Whitebait
Chilled melon
Ravioli au gratin
Grilled fresh sardines

We first have to work out how these dishes can be ready for eating in, say, ten minutes. We can then attempt to identify any risks.

The first starter, avocado vinaigrette, will simply be assembled from an imported whole avocado and a vinaigrette sauce, probably (but not necessarily) bought in. It matters little how either of these items has been stored, since the inside of an unopened fruit should be safe, and no bacteria should grow in vinegar. If the avocado is a creamy-green colour, the fruit has only recently been cut into two; it will be completely safe. The next item, avocado with prawns, is also acceptable as long as the prawns are safe – they should have been washed carefully, so any hepatitis virus, listeria or Vibrio bacteria have been removed. The next item, duck pâté with brown toast, may be riskier. The toast will present no problem; it is the pâté that is questionable. A newly opened tin should be safe, but the flavour may not appeal. If the restaurant has bought in the pâté, the quality is as good as the supplier, but this can be affected by bad storage in the restaurant. If the restaurant makes its own pâté, prolonged storage (say, for more than five days) at high temperatures (e.g. 10 °C) could result in danger. During storage the colour of pâté can darken, and the top can become hard, but the top can easily be shaved off, and the customer will have no idea of its age. This item is entirely a matter of trust.

'Soup of the day' is a convenient phrase; the restaurant does not have to commit itself to a specific flavour in advance. This could be good or bad for the customer: good if, for example, fresh soup is made that day; bad if the restaurant uses the soup as a vehicle for dumping unusable left-overs on the unsuspecting customer. With soup the key is the source. Recently heated, tinned and powdered soups should be safe but will give away their origins in their taste and colours. Some soups are mixtures of commercial soups and fresh additives. Home-produced soup has to be made in advance (that day, with luck) and kept chilled.

Egg mayonnaise is, of course, fraught with danger, not just from salmonella in undercooked eggs but also from the mayonnaise if raw eggs have been used. Some mayonnaise is made from pasteurized eggs (cooked for two and a half minutes at 64.4 °C); this, it is hoped, will contain no salmonella. In addition to salmonella, mayonnaise may, if mistreated by storage at room temperature after opening, be contaminated with *Staphylococcus aureus*. I would not touch egg mayonnaise.

The next item, pancakes *à la maison*, sounds appealing but is made from a number of items and must be produced either in the restaurant or elsewhere in advance. Scrupulous hygiene in its making and storage could ensure safety, but any abuse of these could cause problems, particularly on account of the cream. Caution here!

The whitebait will probably be deep-frozen. It will have to be prepared just before serving and should be safe, as will be the melon.

The ravioli may well be tinned with added cheese. If not, view it as you would the pancake.

The sardines should be safe. In summary, the safest starter items are fresh or deep frozen and prepared just before serving. The more dangerous starters are those that have been processed and prepared in advance.

The next course is a choice of fish:

> Fried breadcrumbed scampi
> Scampi provençal
> Grilled rainbow trout

Salmon, poached, grilled or baked
Fried breaded plaice
Fried haddock in batter
Fisherman's basket – a mixture of prawns, squid,
scampi, pieces of whiting and eel dipped in batter,
fried and served with hollandaise sauce

The fried scampi, the grilled trout, all the salmon, the plaice and the haddock should be safe microbiologically and good nutritionally. Some of these will be deep-frozen, such as the scampi; others, such as the trout, will be fresh. None has been processed. The scampi provençal – pieces of scampi in a cream sauce with various additions – has probably been prepared in advance. The fish in the 'Fisherman's basket' is probably frozen, but, in view of the small size of the pieces, they should be safe. The hollandaise sauce is another matter – it contains egg yolks!

The main course offers a good choice:

Fillet steak (rare, medium or well-done)
Rump steak (rare, medium or well-done)
Châteaubriand (for two people,
rare, medium or well-done)
Steak tartare (raw slices of fillet
in a tartar sauce)
Duck à l'orange
Chicken provençal
Fricassee of turkey
Roast venison
Casserole of hare
Braised pigeon
Roast pork, apple sauce

Gammon and pineapple
Roast lamb, mint sauce

Each is served with a selection of seasonable vegetables
or mixed salad, with a choice of potatoes — new,
chipped, baked or croquette.

The first three items are all steaks, and the usual
options of cooking method are offered to the customer.
This indicates that the steaks are freshly cooked to
order. There should be no problem here. But is raw
steak (steak tartare) safe? I would not risk it. The next
nine items are likely to have been prepared in advance,
often some days before, kept refrigerated or possibly
frozen, to be reheated when required. As far as food
safety goes, there must be a risk, albeit small. The
quality of the sliced beef, pork and lamb is likely to
suffer more than, say, the casserole of hare.

The vegetables should not present any particular
risks, although they may have been stored warm for an
hour or two before serving.

Many menus now also offer a few vegetarian items. I
am told that these are often of poor quality in many restaurants, and very few are made in the restaurant itself.

The sweet choice is as follows:

Fresh fruit salad and cream
Meringues and cream
Bread-and-butter pudding
Apple pie and cream
Crêpes to order
Trifle with cream and custard
The cheese board — selection of English,
French and Swiss cheeses

With four items cream is included. If this has been pasteurized and stored correctly, it should be safe. The fresh fruit poses no problem, and any salmonella in the egg whites in the meringues should have perished during the prolonged cooking. Moreover, the presence of sugar in the meringues also helps to kill any salmonella. All the other sweets contain items from more than one source and, like the starter pancakes, may pose a risk if abuse of temperature and storage has occurred.

The hard cheeses present few problems. The risk of listeriosis from soft cheeses, such as brie and camembert, suggests that vulnerable people avoid these. An ideal meal from the point of view of safety (but not price!) could be chilled melon, fried breaded scampi, medium-cooked fillet steak with fried potatoes, sprouts and carrots, and fruit salad and cream.

TRAINS AND PLANES

Eating while travelling is a unique pleasure, but it is not at all easy for caterers to provide travellers with safe, hot food of a high quality. Both trains and planes employ a certain amount of food that has been prepared and cooked in advance, chilled, stored and transported to the catering area.

On trains and in stations such instant foods include items such as burgers. Each is enclosed in a box printed with a mouth-watering description of the product inside. Unfortunately, the box prevents the buyer from inspecting his intended purchase. The meat fillings in these products have usually been cooked previously; all that is required is reheating in the microwave. After reheating the burger tastes very different from the 'real' burger. The ones I have tasted (what a confession!) were distinctly unpleasant – the buns were soft and flabby rather than firm, and the meat fillings were hard and gritty. But what of their safety? The possible risk comes mainly from the meat. Spores of some food-poisoning bacteria may survive the initial cooking, and many bacteria could contaminate the product after cooking. The conditions of storage between cooking and reheating are extremely important because bacterial growth may not be reliably killed by subsequent micro-wave heating (this was discussed in Chapter 11). The customer has no idea whether the product has been stored under correct refrigeration conditions or how old it is because the carton does not generally show the date of production. I have seen burgers stored in canteens where the refrigeration was certainly inadequate. Inside the glamorous carton is a high-risk food item, and my advice to the reader is to avoid such products on the grounds of poor quality, uncertain nutrition and possible bacterial contamination.

Sandwiches available at stations and in trains are generally made on a daily basis and provide an interesting range. It is regrettable that they are often stored at room temperature. By the afternoon some of the sandwiches may look a little tired, and because each has to be made by hand, and is assembled from several ingredients, contamination (perhaps small) is inevitable. The question of when the product becomes unsafe is impossible to answer. Sandwiches made with egg products, cold chicken and beef may be riskier than, say, those that are cheese based if stored for too long at high temperatures. (Salmonella food poisoning has been associated with egg sandwiches.)

A hot meal on a train may be either produced from raw ingredients there and then or prepared in advance, chilled and transferred to the train. The customer has no idea of the history of his food, whether proper temperature controls have been adhered to or when the food was cooked.

Long-distance plane journeys, during which one or more hot meals really are needed by the passengers, pose catering problems. It is not practicable to cook roast beef and Yorkshire pudding from scratch for 350 passengers on a Boeing 747. Frozen prepared meals require substantial energy to heat them – more than chilled food. It is therefore chilled food that is mainly used. Perhaps the most important factor that affects the safety of airline food is the length of time during which chilled meals are stored – given properly chilled conditions, twenty-four hours should be a risk-free period. If, for example, lunch for the early-morning flight from Heathrow to Los Angeles were prepared the day before, rapidly chilled, plated and kept in ideal temperatures (0–3 °C) before being transferred to the plane in refrigerated lorries at the same temperature, it should be safe. The risk is related to abuse of these exacting requirements in any of the many areas of responsibility through which the food passes.

13

First aid for food poisoning

Having meticulously followed the advice in this book, you should not get food poisoning. But illness could be caused by someone else, and it is impossible to avoid eating everything on social occasions, so let us look at a typical case.

Suppose that all three members of a family, both parents and teenage son, become ill in the early hours of Tuesday morning. They ate similar food the day before. Breakfast was fried bacon and sausages, followed by toast and marmalade. For lunch the principal item was cold lamb left over from Sunday lunch, with new potatoes, carrots, peas and mint sauce. In the evening they met six friends for a minor celebration in a restaurant specializing in oriental food, particularly curries. None of the family feels very ill, but tummy pains and diarrhoea are irritating and uncomfortable. What should they do?

FOUR ESSENTIAL STEPS

The first thing would be to ensure that none of the leftovers or uneaten cooked or raw items were thrown away — neither the refrigerator nor the dustbin should be emptied.

Second, as none of them feels sick, they should sip

water mixed with fruit juice, about half a glass at a time, every half-hour or so.

Third, they should contact the friends they met at the restaurant as soon as possible to find out whether any of them feel under the weather. If not, the illness may have been caused by something that was eaten at home.

Finally, they should telephone their doctor and request a visit from him or her in order to establish the nature of the illness – after all, it may not be food poisoning.

WILL MEDICINES HELP?

If patients feel queasy before the doctor arrives, it would be better for them to visit a chemist and ask the advice of the pharmacist rather than dose themselves with medicine.

Aspirin should not be taken because it can aggravate stomach irritation. Quite a number of preparations of the general 'pick-you-up' variety contain aspirin; while they may be helpful for hangovers, headaches and muscle pains, they are no good for stomach upsets. The spasms of tummy aches will be little helped by aspirin or paracetamol, both of which could do more harm than good.

Some intestinal illnesses are caused by allergies, and antihistamines can be useful in such cases. But if three members of a family become ill at once, the cause is most unlikely to be an allergy, which is very much an individual reaction to a substance. It is possible that one parent and a child could have the same allergy, but the chance of both parents suffering from the same allergy is extremely small.

Milk of magnesia and other remedies that neutralize stomach acid help with disorders that result from too much acid, but some of these medicines can actually cause diarrhoea. A stronger pain killer, such as nurofen, might work, but this acts mainly by lessening muscle pains in the body, not spasms in the guts, and it can upset the stomach.

Antibiotics usually have no value because by the time you are ill the toxin has already damaged you, so it is too late to destroy the bacteria making the toxin. There is also a possibility that antibiotics prolong the length of time a person becomes a carrier of salmonella after recovering from the acute illness.

Alcohol will make matters worse, and the merits of herbal remedies are extremely doubtful.

There is, however, one product that might help the diarrhoea – loperamide. This drug is fairly safe in the right dose and when used for not too long. It will not actually affect the progress of the food-poisoning illness itself, which has resulted from the damaging effect of the bacterial toxins, but it will probably reduce the frequency of the diarrhoea and perhaps that of the colic by lessening the muscular contractions in the intestines. Otherwise the only treatment that is helpful is the replacement, by frequent drinking, of lost fluid.

THE DOCTOR AND THE ENVIRONMENTAL HEALTH OFFICER

A doctor will have two aims when he or she visits a patient who is suffering from acute diarrhoea: to gauge the severity of the illness and to identify its possible cause. If causes other than food poisoning can generally be eliminated – if the patient has not recently been in contact with people who appeared to be suffering from the same complaint, does not have a sore throat and has not had a recent cold – the doctor will want to know what, and where, the patient has eaten over the last two days. (Two days is the longest time that will elapse before the symptoms of food poisoning become apparent – except in the case of listeriosis, which may take up to six weeks to emerge.) The doctor will take specimens and alert the local Environmental Health Department, and an officer will later remove suspect food from the patient's home and from any restaurant or food outlet that could be implicated. It is wise not to warn a restaurant of an impending visit from environmental health officers: this could give it an opportunity to dispose of dangerous food. The tracking of suspect food is essential. In the short term it is necessary to prevent anyone else from eating the food; in the longer term it is very important to correct faulty practices that result in contaminated food.

PRECAUTIONS DURING RECOVERY

The treatment of food poisoning is essentially a matter of waiting for the illness to settle on its own. It is important to drink lots of fluids, and fruit juices are particularly good because they are rich in potassium. While recovering from food poisoning, be meticulous about safe eating. It is absolutely essential not to eat any more suspect food. There is no evidence that immunity to food poisoning builds up, so each time contaminated food is eaten there is a risk. This means that you should not eat out at any restaurant you may have visited in the two days before becoming ill, and at home you should not eat any food of the sort that you have eaten in the last forty-eight hours. A second bout of food poisoning in a weakened person could be very dangerous.

During the days after the attack the diarrhoea should lessen. Washing your hands thoroughly after going to the toilet is even more essential than usual, and if you are the only member of the family who is ill – say, after attending a party – it is a good idea to have your own scrubbing brush, soap and towel, so there is no opportunity for any food-poisoning bacteria in your intestines to be transferred to other people.

GETTING BACK TO WORK

The question of fitness for work will depend on how you feel generally. The exhaustion entailed by food poisoning can last a surprisingly long time. Certainly, any diarrhoea should have ceased before a return to work. If your job involves catering at all – whether the manufacture, distribution, cooking or serving of food – it is essential to report your illness to a responsible person. The same applies to those involved in patient care. If the disease has been identified as salmonella, workers in health care and catering will probably be excluded from contact with patients or food until salmonella has been shown to be absent from three different specimens. They may be told to remain at home, or they may be transferred to a different type of work if that is practical. Fortunately, the prolonged carriage of salmonella for many months is not common, but it does illustrate that the true cost of food poisoning – which is so easily preventable – can be very high.

14

Who protects you, the consumer?

By now you are probably thinking, 'Does anyone?' The consumer in the UK has had a poor deal, and this country has some catching up to do if it wants to match standards and controls in other countries.

At present food is one of the responsibilities of the Ministry of Agriculture, Fisheries and Food (MAFF). The Ministry was set up during the Second World War, when the main problem was food shortages – very different from the problem of today! MAFF has the daunting job of protecting interests of farmers, the fishing industry, food-processing companies, retail outlets and consumers. Some people now argue that the interests of one group cannot be served by a single Ministry without detriment to another group. (For example, on the question of eggs contaminated with salmonella, the protection of egg sales on behalf of the egg producer may conflict with the interest of the egg eater – the consumer.) Others, including the Minister, argue that it makes sense to retain responsibility of every stage of food production in one administrative unit. I sense that many people would welcome the establishment of a watchdog agency that would ensure food safety and would prefer such an agency to be independent of the MAFF. Some have suggested the establishment of a Ministry of Food; others propose an organization totally separate from any government department. The Department of Health also has some responsibility for food safety and acts in an advisory capacity for the public and the MAFF. There is scope for clashes of opinion between the two ministries over action that should be taken to solve a problem, which is one reason for removing responsibility for food safety from ministerial control.

The Acts of Parliament that can be used to enforce food safety are few and, in general, vague. One applies to the pasteurization of milk – that is, the heating of milk at 71·7 °C for at least fifteen seconds. Others involve the safe manufacture of ice cream and the pasteurization of liquid eggs. There is a series of codes of practice that are entirely voluntary (for example, those concerning hygiene in the bakery trade and poultry dressing and packing). Both the Acts and the codes of practice were introduced in response to specific problems and are usually implemented reluctantly. The whole approach to food safety in the UK rests with the food industry: it is self-regulating. Criticism of food safety must therefore be levied at the food industry itself and at the successive governments that have condoned self-regulation. Cynics argue that the food industry eliminates contamination from food only when it has to and, in general, does the minimum required to maintain sales. In the future, unless new legislation is introduced and is shown to be effective, pressures on the food industry may mount so that it will have to take safety issues more seriously.

In practical terms, who is responsible for ensuring that our food is safe? This responsibility rests generally with each local council's Environmental Health Department. This is a pyramidal structure headed by a Chief Environmental Health Officer, who has extensive training in, and wide experience of, environmental health. The department is also responsible for other aspects of public health – for example, pollution by smell, gases, noise, rodents or wasps and certain matters related to housing. The department is advised by a doctor who has special training in these areas and, if there is a problem with food, by the local public health laboratory.

Environmental health officers become involved with food safety in three ways: as a result of a food-poisoning incident, through routine checking and in response to complaints by members of the public, a part of their work that we have not considered so far. Anyone who visits a restaurant or shop and thinks that the standard of the food presented or stored is not high enough or that the premises are a cause for concern can make a complaint directly to the local Environmental Health Department by telephone, in writing or in person. The department is open during office hours, so if an evening meal is thought to be unsatisfactory, it will be the next morning before a complaint can be made. Keep any evidence very carefully. For instance, if you are served with meat in an advanced state of decomposition in a restaurant – that is, if it is putrid and has a revolting smell – put it in a clean container and keep it in the refrigerator until you complain. If you do intend to complain, it is probably not advisable to tell the establishment, as it could cover its tracks before being inspected.

The attitude of the Environmental Health Department to a complaint or any other lapses of hygiene it detects will depend on the circumstances. A prosecution is unlikely to be brought on account of one lapse, which is not too dangerous, in otherwise well-run premises. When lapses occur repeatedly, however, and the management and staff fail to implement improvements after being instructed to do so, prosecution will follow. The simultaneous discovery of a large number of hygiene errors could also result in a court case. Of particular concern would be food left out at warm temperatures, broken refrigerators, the contamination of food (even the possibility of contamination) by animal and human excreta, the presence of flies and larvae, inadequate personal hygiene among the staff, particularly dirty hands, or an outbreak of food poisoning.

After the first complaint and inspection the officers may issue warnings, advice, and indeed, help, or they may request the establishment to cease trading until it has put its house in order. If this request is refused, a court order can be sought and is usually granted. If prosecution does occur, the Environmental Health Department will usually proceed through a magistrates' court, and the officers and members of the public will support the prosecution as witnesses. The defendants are, of course, free to present witnesses and evidence in their favour and to appeal against an adverse verdict. Generally, the Environmental Health Department does not initiate a prosecution unless it is confident that the case will succeed, so as a rule their actions result in penalties imposed on the company involved. In the case of first offences the fines themselves are not generally devastating for the restaurant or shop, but business may well be affected by reports in local papers. (Incidentally, I have never heard of a prosecution being brought against someone whose food, prepared at home, subsequently poisoned family or friends, but it could happen.)

Prosecution against the suppliers of contaminated food (farmers, for example) also seems unusual. Following a spate of claims by many shops and farms that their eggs were guaranteed salmonella-free, it was Trading Standards Officers who acted, not Environmental Health Departments.

In theory, the public is protected by the local council. The problem is that the whole operation is underfunded at all stages. There are inadequate numbers of officers at all grades, particularly those highly trained in food safety. Their powers depend on the threat of prosecution or actual application to the courts. Batches of suspect food are difficult to confiscate. Moreover, much food microbiology is done by the government's own Public Health Laboratory service. Some of the laboratories have close ties with big industrial concerns and may not be keen to aid prosecutions against them. There is also inadequate independent testing of food at the point of purchase. It is true that food is regularly tested for bacterial contamination by all the major companies before distribution, but this does not ensure safety, since contamination and the growth of bacteria can occur after distribution – for, example, listeria may appear to be absent from a recipe meal tested just after production, but it may be present when you eat the food.

The need for this book is a reflection of the fact that at present our food-safety monitoring is simply not good enough. This is not the fault of those who are charged with responsibility for it: their numbers, their powers and their terms of reference are inadequate. There is an urgent need for new legislation and a tough, independent agency with which those who are now involved with environmental health, and food safety in particular, could liaise.

Meanwhile, the onus is on us all to avoid food poisoning.

15
The future

INTENSIVE FARMING PRACTICES AND THEIR CONSEQUENCES

The rate at which farming practices have been changing has been quite remarkable. Intensive rearing methods have been developed only over the last fifty years. Inevitably, the way in which animals are reared for food production must determine the quality and safety of the meat. Intensive rearing is now the norm, rather than the exception, for broiler chickens, egg-laying chickens, turkeys, ducks and pigs. The farming of salmon and trout is being developed, though parasitic and bacterial infections still occur in the fish. Cattle spend a proportion of their life in enclosed sheds, and even deer are being reared specially for food. It is only sheep that are free to roam the countryside. These changes in husbandry are not necessarily to be deplored, but they have brought in their wake new problems that require solutions. The spread of *Salmonella enteritidis*, for example, can be viewed as one consequence of specialized breeding, intensive rearing and the recycling of chicken remains in feed. It can be combated, but both the elimination of salmonella from the flocks in the first place and monitoring to prevent a recurrence in the future will be expensive.

Bovine spongiform encephalopathy (BSE), dubbed 'mad cow disease' by the media, is another disturbing and distasteful side-effect of new farming methods. (Those of you who wish to continue to enjoy beef should perhaps skip the next section.)

The first cases of BSE were diagnosed in 1985, and since that time the incidence has increased each year. Infected cattle become anxious and frightened; they are unsteady on their feet and often walk with a swaying of the back legs. They may become violent. The amount of milk produced drops. The animals usually have to be destroyed. Only adult cows, usually between three and six years old, are affected. By the end of 1988 about 2,000 cases had been identified in the UK. (Oddly, BSE does not appear to have been described outside the UK, though it is possible that it has not been looked for carefully.)

The cause of the disease is a tiny infectious element, which may be a protein or a nucleic acid. It is much smaller even than a virus, so several thousands may be packed into a bacterium. In infected cows it is the brain that is damaged: the term spongiform encephalopathy refers to the sponge-like appearance of a diseased brain.

Considerable research has been done on the factors associated with this disease. There is no evidence of the transmission of the disease between cattle, so the movement of infected cattle among herds is not the cause. What is certain, however, is that the disease is transferred via recycled animal protein in the cows' feed, particularly during the winter. There are about forty factories in the UK that process the waste products of animals, such as bones, heads and intestines. This is known as 'rendering'. Two final products are fat for industrial purposes, such as the manufacture of soap for human use, and protein that is added to animal feed. Few infectious agents will survive rendering, but the infectious agent of BSE appears to be very resistant to heat and chemicals. There is strong evidence that animal residues infected with the agent that causes BSE are being processed and fed to cattle. What animal is the likely source? The answer is sheep, which have been known for many years to suffer occasionally from a similar brain disease called scrapie. The rendering of sheeps' brains is the most likely cause of BSE in cattle.

If only 2,000 cattle out of hundreds of thousands have been infected by BSE, is it really a serious matter? Unfortunately, yes – very serious. The real worry for the human population is the risk of catching BSE from infected animals. A rare brain disease in human beings, Creutzfeldt–Jacob disease, has been known for some years and is similar to BSE in cattle and scrapie in sheep. Perhaps the most reassuring fact is that while scrapie has been occurring in sheep for many years, there is no proof that we can catch it. BSE in cattle is too new for us to be certain that we cannot catch it from infected cows, although that is unlikely. Nevertheless, a number of important actions have already been taken. The most important is the BSE Order of 1988, which prohibits the sale of some animal residues and their use as feed for cattle. Other measures have also been taken to protect the human population from the risk of infected meat products.

It cannot be a coincidence that *Salmonella enteritidis* and BSE have only recently emerged as problems: they must inevitably be associated with modern farming practices. There are some lessons for us to learn from them.

The first is that we should not progress towards more intensive farming at present; rather, we should return animals to open spaces, which would both contribute to soil fertility and reduce the risk of infection between animals.

Second, we should not recycle the remains of dead animals in the feed of living ones, particularly when the live animals are herbivores. The natural diet of cows is grass, not treated sheeps' heads.

Third, the monitoring of intensely reared animals and birds must increase. We require more research, more veterinary surgeons and more inspections. At the moment government policy seems to be proceeding in exactly the opposite direction.

Fourth, meat and poultry are probably as cheap now as they ever will be. Essential controls will raise prices slightly.

Fifth, if we improve the safety of our intensely reared animals and birds in the UK, British farmers will probably be hard-pressed to compete with certain imports. Food safety must, therefore, be treated internationally.

It is not my intention to suggest that we should return to the Middle Ages or that each household should own two cows, a few sheep, a goat and a pig. The point is that we should be aware that intensive farming methods have developed very rapidly and are now raising problems that will have to be solved – at a price.

TRENDS IN SHOPPING

In Chapter 8 we saw how our shopping habits had changed over the years. Now a weekly or even less frequent visit to a supermarket enables us to buy all our food, but perishable goods have to survive for longer than they should. There are two alternatives: to add preservatives to these products or to risk bacterial contamination. We can eat either additives or bacteria! The food items in question are meat, fish, poultry, some vegetables and certain processed or convenience meals. Supermarkets are a source of readily available, inexpensive food; for non-perishable products, such as dried, canned or preserved food, they will continue to offer good value. But we should supplement our basic requirements with fresh produce from local shops several times a week, and we should demand suitable local outlets.

INSTITUTIONAL CATERING

The feeding of a large number of patients, children or staff in an institution has always been difficult. While it is fairly straightforward to cook food in bulk in a central kitchen, it is much harder to serve it hot. During distribution in trolleys the temperature of the food falls, and there is a loss of both flavour and taste. Moreover, feeding a large number of people at the same time requires a large staff for fairly limited periods, so the use of labour is inefficient.

One attempt to circumvent these problems was adoption of the cook–freeze system, whereby food is cooked in bulk, deep frozen rapidly to between $-18\,°C$ and $-23\,°C$ and stored in portions ready for reheating and serving where it is to be eaten. This sounds fine in theory, but difficulties arise in connection with the reheating and distribution. Consider a hospital with a central kitchen and, say, thirty wards and a staff canteen. For each meal about 800 patients and 400 staff will have to be fed. The options open are to reheat the food in the central kitchen and distribute it warm, as with conventional catering, or to reheat it in each ward and in the canteen. With central reheating the costs are low, and custards, gravies and soups can be transported to the wards in bulk in containers within the trolleys. However, by the time the patients receive the food its quality may be poor, as reheated frozen food deteriorates very rapidly when it is kept hot. If food is reheated at ward level, on the other hand, it has to be transported in the frozen state, then reheated in fairly expensive ovens in ward kitchens. Moreover, custards, gravies and soups must be made in each ward. The cost of reheating and serving at ward level is very high.

Cook–chill catering presents the same dilemma and is associated with greater risks because bacteria such as listeria can flourish under chilled conditions. The Department of Health's 1980 guidelines on the safe operation of cook–chill catering state that reheating should take place 'at the point of consumption' and that the food should be consumed 'immediately'. These recommendations are not compatible with reheating in central kitchens, yet, according to a 1988 survey of the Institute of Environmental Health Officers, more than half of the hospitals in the UK that operate a cook–chill system reheat the chilled food centrally, in existing kitchens, thus contravening the Department's own guidelines. The only explanation is that in the minds of certain hospital managers cook–chill is the only way to privatize catering, a procedure more important, apparently, than the provision of quality food or ensuring the safe operation of the system.

The National Health Service and other types of institutional catering must surely consider the following points.

First, are three hot meals daily really necessary?

Second, conventional catering should be revived and improved. There should be more, smaller kitchens and better distribution trolleys (some of the new trolleys are extremely well insulated).

Third, the catering system selected must be the one that is most appropriate for a particular unit, and it should not be introduced primarily as a means of privatization.

At the time of writing many hospitals are being designed and built with no production kitchens. Food will have to be supplied by the private sector, using cook–chill procedures. It is difficult to see how this expedient can comply with the Department of Health's guidelines or how it can be monitored adequately for safety. In the UK the cook–chill catering system has never been properly evaluated for safety, nutrition, palatability or total costs by comparison with other systems.

The requirement of local authorities to put their school meals out to competitive tender could generate problems similar to those of the Health Service.

COOKING AND CATERING AT HOME

Finally, let's return to the home and the individual. If recent trends in eating habits continue, we will be eating our food while on the run – literally. In the evening our city streets are invaded by walking burger-eaters who drop fatty onion on the pavement, by fried chicken on the move, by the march of fish and chips through doorways. The leisure society is here to stay, but we must appreciate that the provision of instantly available food carries inherent risks, and we must put more effort into safeguarding convenience foods.

At home we should resist the tyranny of television schedules. We should give meals more time, respect and status. We should look beyond the advertising men and the costly, glamorous packages that give an illusion of quality; instead we should buy raw ingredients of real quality and prepare the meals we want rather than those thrust on us by the suppliers of frozen and cook–chill products. (I know of a brewery that intends to produce pre-cooked chilled food for reheating in pubs. Only a narrow range of items is amenable to this treatment: they include pasta dishes, *chilli con carne* and potted pies. *But are they what we all want?*)

If you follow the advice in this book, you will be doing your utmost to prevent food poisoning in yourself, your family and your visitors. Enjoy your food.

Index

171

INDEX